The Greatest Gift

The Greatest Gift

Gertrude Mattingly Banks

PALMETTO

P U B L I S H I N G

Charleston, SC

www.PalmettoPublishing.com

Hardcover ISBN: 9798822954977
Paperback ISBN: 9798822954984
eBook ISBN: 9798822954991

Gertrude's family would like to thank everyone
who were so encouraging about her writing so many
beautiful poems, stories, and articles through the years.

This is the first novel that I have worked hard on to get
ready for publication. With the help of granddaughter,
K'Lynn Ferguson, handling the technical part with
the publisher, it is finally ready!

Hope everyone, especially young people, will read
and enjoy knowing how their grandparents coped
with the very hard times back in their day.

Contents

Chapter 1

Amanda was getting more worried every second that the new 1932 Chevrolet sedan she was riding in would turn over as it came back up to the town square and made all four corners on two wheels. Boyd Chalmers never stopped, not even for a second, so there was no chance for Amanda to slide out the front opening back door of the car and run for safety. After careening around the corners of the square, the group screamed and did catcalls, and everybody took another round from the half-gallon fruit jar. Howard had told her, in a whisper, to put the jar up to her mouth and pretend to sip it, and he seemed to be doing the same. The more times the jar made the rounds, the louder the other four people got with their screaming and merrymaking. Then, the next time the fruit jar came to Amanda, somebody pushed up from the bottom of the fruit jar, spilling the sharp and choking fumes down her chin and the front of her shirt as she was trying to fake a sip of the vile stuff.

She choked and coughed, and the crowd laughed and hooted louder, and it seemed everything got funnier to everyone except for her and Howard Huff. As time passed and her troubles got more frightening, Amanda became petrified that *if* and *when* the crowd did agree to take her home, her daddy, J. M. Mason, would be awake and would shoot first and ask questions later. The very thought of his 30-30 gun and his awful temper and cussing fits made her realize she had to get away from the crowd because the drunken bunch would spell nothing but doom at her house. If she was lucky enough to keep them quiet enough to get to the house, her daddy would take one look at her, smell the rotgut whisky on her, and probably beat her to death. Then there was the surety that, if and when Boyd left her house, his motor would be wide open. He would make it do the loud popping noises like he always did tonight, when he made the four corners of the square with the tires squealing and the bunch screaming on the way out of town.

The girls became the loudest of the group, and as they got to the square one time, one of them was yelling to the houses, "Get up, you SOBs. It's time to milk." She was not using initials, and Amanda was horrified and wanted to die. "Where in the world are the lawmen?" she asked herself. She dreaded being caught with this bunch, but she had heard enough to realize that what they planned for her was too awful to contemplate. The other girls began to taunt her, saying how goody-goody she thought she was, but soon, they promised, she would know what real fun was.

Now, she knew, was the time to make her move as the put-putting car clonked slowly up Canard Street. So she told Howard good-bye and begged him to open the door quietly and let her go. This was the first time she had gone anywhere with any of the town kids, and she was sure that whether she lived or not, it would be her last time. As quietly as he could, Howard opened the door, and Amanda crawled across his knees and fell to the graveled street.

At first she thought she could not get up, but she realized she had to, as she was not yet free of the drunken bunch. She had to hide from them until she could take the woods trail to her house. She knew if she could get into the woods, she might have a chance, as she knew every bush, every tree, and every gully. She walked it every day from home to school, and from school and Mr. C. H. Connor's store every evening.

Her tired brain became aware the car was making the corners of the square again, so she stood and ran, or hopped on her right leg and dragged her left one. She had to get through the alley and to the right to get to the back of Connor's store. Now was the crucial time as she heard the shotgun-sounding pops as the car left the square.

She made it to the back of the store, but she could not consider trying to open the doors, as the car would be here before she could open the lock on the chain and get inside. She crawled under the loading ramp that ran from the alley to the covered porch, at the back of the store, and wedged under the very lowest boards. She hoped Mr. Connor had locked the doors at the back of the building as he left to go home, as the key to the chain lock back here was the only one she had. If he had closed these doors and left from the front, there would be a two-by-four across the double doors, and the key in her pocket would do her no good whatsoever. Right now, the only hope she had was that this store could be a sanctuary—the only place of safety she could think of in the whole town.

The space under the ramp was damp and smelly from the years the garbage barrel had sat on the ramp, and she felt sick from the awful odor. Then she became paralyzed as she saw the car lights wavering across the back of the building. The lights were flickering across her as they slowly entered the alley. The car stopped, and she cowered there and prayed they would not find her in her hiding place.

Boyd was cursing and sneering at Howard for helping his "date" escape and robbing everybody of the fun they could have had, he said, from getting Amanda drunk enough so they could initiate her into the real fun of dating. "Then the prissy slut could have known how to enjoy herself on dates," he said.

Then, for the first time, Howard took issue for her. He explained that even if Amanda was country and maybe a little goody-goody, he was really not for keeping on with this kind of stuff, as Boyd and the other boy already had dates that loved a good time.

Then Boyd said, "You don't have a date now, so we'll take you back to the creek bottom, where the class is having the stew." Then he lowered his voice and said, "We'll pretend we're leaving town and then come back here to sneak up on her when she thinks we're gone."

With squealing tires and flying gravel, he took off back up to the square and took the north road out of town. He poured on the speed for a bit; then he stopped, and she could hear them all unloading and starting to run back up to town. She unwound her stiff and aching body, dragged herself onto the ramp, and prayed the two-by-four on the inside was not across the doors. If the door was locked from the inside, she might as well give up. She pulled the heavy chain with the big lock down and turned the key. It worked, and she unhooked it and pushed on the right-hand door. It gave, and she breathed a prayer of thanks as she edged her body through the opening she had made; there was just a little space to allow her to get inside and gently lay the two-by-four into the slots on both doors.

No sooner had she accomplished this than she heard Boyd and Howard outside, looking under the ramp with a flashlight. Boyd said, "That little bitch ain't going to get away with this. I'll find her, if not tonight, then sometime."

Then Howard said, "You know, Boyd, I like to have a good time as much as anybody, and I take what's offered, you know that, but I'm not for stuff like this. In the first place, it's not right, and it's dangerous. You can get killed pretty quick by a girl's daddy or boyfriend."

"Yeah, yeah, we know that, but you're not in our crowd. You were along tonight because you were the only one that could get the little snotty bitch to come along. You're a little bit of a goody-goody yourself, and this story better not be told around town, as you know there's a lot of ways to make people suffer. A lot of ways…"

The threat was there in those words, and Amanda felt fear crawl up her arms and legs to the depths of her mind and her heart. Fear for herself and Howard Huff—the only person in school who had offered her a hesitant friendship.

Then Howard said, "So your bunch did gang rape the poor little cross-eyed Manning girl. I heard it, but I didn't believe it. Don't you all feel a little bit of a question and shame that there is a baby out there somewhere that looks like one or the other of you?"

"Hell, yes, there may be twins or maybe triplets that look like different ones of us. Wouldn't that be a killer!" And he roared with laughter—sneering laughter. Then the boys moved on.

Amanda saw then that she was shaking so hard, her teeth were chattering so loud, that she wondered why the boys had not heard them while they were right outside the doors.

She knew the store so well she needed no more lights than the one single bulb that hung from the ceiling and always stayed on in the front part of the store. She made her way to the bathroom and washed her face and hands. She tried to get the caked, smelly dirt from under the loading ramp off her legs and her dress. Then she became violently sick and had to clean herself up again. The nausea, with the bitter-as-bile taste in her mouth and throat, kept her busy for a while.

She was thankful she worked here most days after school and had an idea Mr. Connor would understand why she was here if she told him the story of her first and only date. This was the first social for the town school she had been to, and some social it had turned out to be. When Howard had come to the porch at her house, he had been polite and courteous to her mother and had told her they would be back as soon as the class picnic, which was a squirrel stew, was over.

She moved to where the men's jackets were hanging, pulled one down, and put it on. She knew she had to go home sometime, but not yet, please, God, not yet. Boyd Chalmers was out there some-where...somewhere, and she did not know where.

She sat scrunched up in a chair for a long time, and then, just before dawn, she built a fire in the round-bellied woodstove, swept the floors, and put things in places where they could easily be found by the customers.

She left a note for Mr. C. H. that she had been here but needed to attend to some business. Her hand shook when she wrote the word "business" because she had a terrifying feeling that when she got home, the "business" would turn into tragedy.

The morning was cool, with the touch and feel of frost in the air, and her breath formed puffs of cotton like clouds before her face. It seemed strange to Amanda to be going toward home at this time of the day, as she usually, at this time or soon after, was on the way toward town to make it to school on time. Her shirt was too light to stop the cold breeze that raked across the dewy grass. She shivered from the cold, or maybe from her nerves, because she had no idea what would happen when she got home.

When she crossed the fence in front of the little house that she, her silent mother, and her very vocal father lived in, she saw her daddy coming from the barn toward the house. Then she saw him cut away from the line to the back door and start toward her. He had not only changed directions, but he was walking faster and faster, almost in a run, and she saw his mouth moving furiously. Then she heard the words that were coming out of his mouth. Of all the times she had listened and seen his temper fits, she had never heard such vile language and screeching. Foam was at the corners of his mouth, and she suddenly knew if he got to her, her life would be worthless; she would be doomed.

She had no choice but to crawl back through the fence and keep some distance between them. She was screaming too and was begging him to listen to her for just one minute. He never heard one word she said and was coming toward her faster and faster. Finally, she took to her heels and heard him calling her names: whore, bitch, and strumpet. She did not remember if she had ever heard that last name, but the word *bitch* brought a picture of Boyd Chalmers to her mind. She realized even if she could tell her father what had happened last night, he would never believe she had done everything she could to keep from becoming those awful names he was calling her. When she was almost out of hearing distance, the last words she heard were that he would catch her if he had to run down every animal he had on the place.

It came to her then that her life had changed forever; she had no idea what she could do and how she could survive. Even though the threat of Boyd Chalmers would forever haunt her, she knew going back to the house of her parents was no option. She would have to go there one more time to get the school's books and what few clothes she had. That would be when her father was gone far enough that she could get her things and get across some fences so he could not run her down on his horse.

She would make a visit, a short visit, and maybe her mother would listen to her story of how she had been mistreated and terrified by the town kids. Maybe she could say "goodbye" to her quiet, stolid mother when she went to get her books and things.

She spent hours in the woods, waiting and watching the house to see if her daddy would come into these, the Tiner's woods, to try to hunt her.

It was after the middle of the afternoon when she saw him come from the barn leading his roan gelding. He had managed to keep the gelding when everything in the way of livestock had been sold—everything except his work mules and their cow. He had managed to keep the cow, and that was their main source of healthy food and drink to go with the garden stuff she and her mother raised and put up every year. It all had worked so far, along with their chickens, some pigs, and the game her father hunted in the creek and river bottoms.

Amanda watched from the woods as her daddy mounted the horse and took to the road in front of the house, toward the main road, then turned right at the highway toward town. He let the high-stepping horse hit a fast pace he called a "single-foot." When he and the horse got out of sight, she headed through the open space between the woods and the fence in front of the house. She crossed the fence and flew to the foursquare little house.

Her mother looked up from the churning she was doing, dasher in hand, and laid her book aside.

"Well, this is something that I hoped I would never see. How in the world could you do it? Why in the world would you believe your father would condone such behavior?"

Amanda looked at her mother, and it dawned on her that her mother, just like her father, believed the worst of her and had no intentions of listening to anything she had to say. She would listen to no story about why her child had stayed away from home all night.

"Mother, I can't believe you would think I would do this willingly. What kind of child have I been to cause you both to accept that I am a low-class, easily tempted slut? That was one of the nicer names he called me at the top of his lungs, wasn't it? If that is what you think of your teachings and your own model life, then there is no place for me in this house, your church, and this community."

She swallowed the hurt, blinked back the tears, and stalked back to her small room in a corner of the little foursquare house. She picked up her books and her notebook and took her hanging clothes from behind the door. Then she shook a pillow from a pillowcase and stuffed her underwear from a drawer and the other items into it. When this was accomplished, she went back through to the living room and made for the front door, ready to crawl under the fence to Tiner's woods again. She did not look back, and the feeling of sadness she felt was not for her leaving, but for her mother, who had not stopped the churn dasher or laid her book down this time. She just pronounced, "Amanda, you realize you are ruined forever," as her only child left her only home. Forever? Her mother's words were engraved in her mind and her heart, and were more hurtful than all of her father's raging and profanity. The tears scalded her cheeks as she marched along with the overloaded pillowcase, bumping along at her back. She plodded thorough the post oak trees toward town and a very uncertain future.

It was after closing time when she got back to the store, and for some reason, she felt relieved. If Mr. C. had locked up from the back again, she would not have to go to his home and ask for a key to get into the store. She felt disoriented and hoped she could be alone in the store, as it appeared it was the only safe place for her anymore. She used her key and let herself in. She felt a little better as she hung her clothes up on the rack where the men's work clothes were, and then her stomach rumbled and ached, and she realized she was hungry.

She ate an apple; then, she lost face with herself, as the apple was not enough. Her huger took control, so she ate a banana too. It dawned on her then that she had had no food since yesterday at noon, and that had been her sausage and biscuit from her lunch sack at school.

She felt dirty and sick. Since the stove was still hot, she filled the pan from the bathroom with water and set it on the stove to heat. Trying to fill some time, she took out her books and began to read what had been assigned for the day's lesson in History. She loved history, and she loved to read anything. Anything...period. When the water was warm, she washed herself and thanked the Lord and Mr. Connor for the bar of soap in the bathroom by the tap. Then she pulled out the cot Mr. C. now used to take his rest in the afternoons since his heart attack. The one quilt was a little light to sleep under, so she took down a quilted man's jacket from a rack and dropped it over her feet. She knew it would be cold when the fire went out, but Amanda was exhausted and fell asleep. She mumbled her nightly prayer and felt safe enough and clean enough to lay aside some of her troubles. She could halfway believe maybe the Lord would provide.

Once, during the night, she awoke so cold she put another stick of wood in the stove and went back to sleep. When daylight came she built the fire, swept the floors, and put the produce out. Then she took another apple, cut a slice of cheese, took some crackers from an opened box, and went away to the schoolhouse.

She knew it was too early for the school to be unlocked, so she went to the back, hoping the basement door would be open. It was, and she looked around for the janitor; then she crept down to the girl's bathroom, went into one of the stalls, and locked the door. She waited there until the first bell. She felt guilty because she had not called Mr. Connor and owned up to all the things that were happening to her. But her brain was in a perpetual foment, and nothing was clear to her now. How was she to explain the upheaval in her life and make sense of how everything had happened in so short a time—to alter everything she was familiar with and leave herself homeless and destitute?

When she went upstairs to study hall and then on to her first class, she felt a little relieved. Maybe she could continue on in school if Mr. C. H. would let her sleep in the store at night. Then, when her first class was ending, Mr. Donaldson, the principal, met her in the hall and asked her to accompany him to his office. There he questioned her about her absence the day before and asked for her excuse from her parents. She told him her father was away and her mother was sick. She said that in the rush to do all the chores and get everything done to be able to leave her mother, they had both forgotten the excuse.

She had found herself making up the story as she went along. She knew she was not good at lying and was a little surprised when the principal accepted her feeble excuse.

At any rate, she made it to her classes, turned in papers for the assignments she had missed the day before, and did some makeup work for today's classes. She had always loved school and been a good student. She was one of the few students to enter the high school here from a little, common school district who did not have to repeat any of the grades or the work. She had not been behind the pupils who had been in the Canesville schools through all the grades. The main reason she was up in all her courses was her love of reading and studying. She had read and absorbed everything her little school had to offer, and Mrs. Groce, the teacher, had brought as many books as she could from her home, from the library, and from her friends to keep Amanda busy and interested.

When school was over for the day, Amanda walked to town and very hesitantly entered the Connor Store. Mr. C. H. spoke to her as he always did, turned his customer, whom he was checking out, over to her, and went to the back to watch Mr. Pod Green, who was loading his cow feed. She still knew the time was coming when she must tell Mr. C. all the terrible things that had happened to her. She really wanted to tell it to somebody. She had no family who would listen to the sorry tale, and knew no schoolteacher well enough to trust with her problem. The minister of their little country church was an absolute no-no.

If the minister of her mother's church knew there was trouble in her family and mentioned it, her mother might stop going there.

That church, as far as Amanda could see, and its piano were all her mother had to look forward to. Their piano at home was one of the first things that had been sold when the hard times came. So, it was help from Mr. C. H. Connor or leaving town, and how could she leave town with just a few measly dollars in her pocket? She would have even fewer dollars when she paid Mr. C. for the fruit and cheese she had eaten last night and today.

When the last customer was gone and Mr. C. had locked the back and had come up front, he said, "Do you want to tell me about it?"

And of course, she said, "Yes." She told him an abbreviated version of her unhappy date and the wild, drinking bunch of kids in Boyd Chalmers's car. When she got to the point in her story of what happened when she had tried to go home, tears came, and she could not help it. The awful horror of being hunted like an animal, here in town, by an evil Boyd Chalmers and hearing her daddy call her those terrible names and threaten to kill her was too much. It was an overload for her tired and exhausted body and, most of all, her brain. She felt her heart had already solidified into a charred mass.

When Mr. C. heard what she had to say, he asked if it was her father's temper that had caused her to stay in the store again last night. Of course, she said, "Yes." She still felt an unsettled and nameless fear. Mr. C. H.'s hand, with a handkerchief, was holding her tears, and she found herself leaning into his portly body.

Then, Mr. C. turned her so he could see her face and said, "Can I ask you one more question?" And she nodded her head. He said, "Amanda, are you in trouble?"

Then she said, "Oh, Lord, Mr. C., the very worst kind." And she did not see the sadness on the dear man's face.

His day was over, so he set the lock on the door and said, "You can sleep here again tonight, but for goodness' sake, keep a fire in the stove and eat a meal across the street." Then he handed her some money and said, "Tomorrow we will do what we need to do to fix it so you will be under my protection...from that day forward. Will that be OK with you?" And she dumbly nodded. Then he gave her a key to the front door and said, "Good night, Amanda." And he left.

She felt assured but puzzled. What in the world had he meant when he said she would be under his protection from...that day forward? That had sounded almost like a ritual of some kind, she mused. And how was she going to be kept safe? She could not be with him all the time. She had to go to school, and Boyd Chalmers would be there. He had promised, in her hearing, he would find her, and she could almost feel the awful things he had in store for her. Then why had Mr. C. asked if she was in trouble, when she had just told him about all the awful things that were happening to her?

She did not eat across the street at Minningers. She felt the only safe place she had in this world was in this building. Outside, she would be terrified Boyd Chalmers was right behind her. That he would hunt her down like an animal; that he would pounce at any second. She wondered if she would ever be free from that fear as long as she lived.

She made and ate a peanut-butter-and-banana sandwich, drank a Grapette soda water, stoked up the fire, and went to sleep.

She was surprised when she awoke that Mr. C. was building up the fire in the stove beside the cot. He was early. Then she remembered he had said this was the day when he would do what needed to be done to make things right, and oh Lord, she hoped he could.

In the bathroom she washed herself, put on one of her school dresses, and combed her hair. Then she heard Mr. C. talking to someone and listened, as she knew it was too early for a customer. She realized he was talking to Thomas McGraed. McGraed was the man from out at Sidings Crossing who had worked when Mr. C. had his heart attack. She had worked with him quite a bit last summer, and they had gotten along quite well. She wondered if he was here to work while Mr. C. was out somewhere trying to find her a place to live. She wondered what place there was that she would be under his protection and safe. She shook her head and waited and wondered.

Then Mr. C. walked back to her, looked at her, and she could see wheels turning in his head, and she wondered what he was trying to work out. Then he said, "Little lady, put on your best bib and tucker, and let's get this show on the road."

The blood rushed to her face and head, and she felt she could faint. Then she turned, took down her navy blue church dress, and went into the bathroom to put it on. She went back to the pillow-case, took out her stockings and low-heel pumps, and put them on. When she stood in front of him, she was so giddy with shame and embarrassment she wanted to run out the door, and go, and go... and go.

Then Mr. C. patted her on the shoulder and said, "Might fine. Mighty fine. I guess we are ready for the big event."

She wanted to ask, "What big event is that?" But she did not ask, and she wondered many times afterward why she had not.

She sat in the big automobile beside the finest man she had ever known. She felt her brain was hung up there somewhere above her head and was not working. It just was up there doing nothing—in limbo. Her mouth was dry, and her eyes were only moving once in a while, when a conscious command from an addled brain told them to move.

There was a layer of morning fog that surrounded the big car and its occupants as it ate up the miles. It was not long until they crossed the Red River into Oklahoma. Finally, Amanda could stand it no longer and got up her nerve to try to squeak out a question. She cleared her throat and asked, "Where are we going?" Her voice was still squeaky, but she knew he heard her.

Then he looked at her, mumbled something, and pulled to the side of the road and stopped. His face was red, maybe as red as hers had been when he had told her to change her dress. He looked completely awash in embarrassment and tried to make his voice work and to apologize, but it took a few minutes.

"Amanda, I am so sorry. I guess I thought you could read my mind. I guess when I told you I would take care of you, you would know what I meant. But how do you think you would be under my protection any other way? I meant we would be married. Is that all right with you? Do you want to go back home? I will do whatever you say."

He looked so crestfallen she reached out a hand, touched his arm, and said, "Mr. C., that is the greatest compliment anyone has ever given me. But why are you taking my troubles and problems on you? Do you want to go through this with me? Why do you want to saddle your free, peaceful, enjoyable life with an ignorant, dumb kid like me? One who has a teenage criminal out to chase her down and a father who is a maniac with murder on his mind?"

"Well, little girl, think a minute. My life has been fine, yet it is nearly over, and I have very little to show for it. Mrs. Leona and I were happy, and she never complained we could not have children, but it was a lonely shock when she left this earth and me. I saw then just how pitifully little my life had to offer. I have tried to make a difference in a few lives, yet I have nobody to settle my little business on when I leave, and I am getting the message I don't have a lot of time left. Can you let me do this thing for you, then…and would you do for me what needs to be done when I am not here? Can you share my last little while and maybe finish some of the projects I have started?" He waited a minute and then continued. "I am sorry I didn't tell you this last night. I really should have, and you would have had time to think about it and the changes it would make in your life. Think about it now, before you answer. Look at it as a momentous, solemn step in your life. And only say 'yes' if you really want to go through with it."

And Amanda nodded her head because she was speechless.

Then he said, "Come to think about it, neither of us has had breakfast, and it is well up in the morning. How about we drive on up to the next little town and find a place to have something to eat?" And Amanda nodded again.

Then Mr. C. turned the car back onto the road, and they were both quiet while they made their way to a little Oklahoma town on a bright, sunshiny day that was cold yet pleasant. Amanda had been enjoying seeing the countryside, and Mr. C. talked a little about the differences in the terrain of Oklahoma and Texas. He pointed out that the river they had just crossed was named Red River for a reason, and she let him know she had noticed it really was red—the banks, the water, and the bluffs up on the Oklahoma side.

When they stopped in front of a small cafe, Amanda said, "Well now, I have seen more of Texas than I have ever seen before, and this is my first glimpse of Oklahoma." She laughed an embarrassed little chuckle, and the wonderful man laughed with her.

When they were seated in the warm, friendly little cafe, Amanda studied the menu and then the main street of the town through the sweat drops on the plate glass window. They ordered, and she found she finally could look at Mr. C. H. without becoming tongue-tied, and said, "Mr. C., you are a wonderful person, and what you are offering me is way, way beyond the call of duty. But you should be thinking too. If we do this, the whole town will go into a big uproar. I have felt some negative vibes already, just by working my few hours each week. It seems some people's idea is that if you were going to give somebody a job with pay, it should have been someone who has a family to feed."

"Amanda, I did my thinking last night, and some praying. If we are going to do this, let's make our plans to honor each other and make my little business…our business. I want everyone to know you will be my wife; you will work with me in the store and learn everything you can about the running of it while I am here. I want you involved with our town. Does that sound all right?"

And Amanda said, "I am ready to do anything you think will work. After all, I am homeless and hopeless, and what you are offering me seems an answer, truly an answer, to my prayers I have been saying for three days now. I am ready to follow you in any way I can."

"I hope you will always be glad we are doing what we plan today." And he smiled at her, and the world seemed a brighter place. "As to why I hired you…You see, if a man has a family, there is food to be had for the asking. It is called 'relief.' You could not qualify; only heads of households can. When I realized how desperately you wanted and needed to go to school, I saw a way to help—not just to help you, but how you could help me in return."

"Mr. C., I can never go back to that place where I lived with those two people. I will never understand why you let me tell you what happened and believed me when neither of my parents would listen to anything I tried to say."

She pushed back from the table and was ready to go before tears could start to fall again. She wondered why she was so lucky to have a friend to bargain with her, like this wonderful man who was willing to bear her burdens with her. She felt she had a friend and comforter, and to her, he was the epitome of goodness and fairness, not just in business but also in all walks of life. That was apparent from his associations and conversations with others.

He seemed to be pondering what she had said last and finally said, "Sometimes people are too close to a situation to be reasonable. Could that have been what happened with your parents?"

"Maybe," she said. "But I have tried to do and be what they wanted me to be. That was the first and only date I have had, and I believed, just as they did, that a class social would be well chaperoned, that I would be home early, because it was a school event on a school night. Also, I had felt a tentative friendship developing between Howard Huff and myself. He seemed as shocked as I was when the others in the car turned into loud, drunken, wild teenagers with no sign of consciences or any awareness of right and wrong."

"But your folks did not let you tell them what happened, and that is a sad shame."

"I don't believe they ever will. It has always seemed they were waiting and watching, knowing I was going to do something bad;

that they knew it was going to happen, they just didn't know when." And she surreptitiously wiped her eyes.

"Whatever mistakes you have made are not the end of the world. They are in the past, and we can go on from here and try to make mistakes into a victory. Right?" And he smiled that wonderful smile that had always made her feel better.

"Yes," she said. "I want to be the very best help I can be in the store and in your life. I feel so flattered you think I can be an asset— as I have always felt I am a liability."

"Amanda, how could you, in any way, have been a liability when you were a hand in your father's fields and did most of the chores?"

She said, "I really don't know, but it appeared, at all times, they felt I was."

"Well, at any rate, if you truly feel you want to do this today, maybe we should be on our way." He took her elbow, ushered her out to the car, and opened the door for her.

When she looked up into his face with a questioning smile, with a big grin on his face, he said, "Get used to this. All ladies should have doors opened for them."

The Oklahoma town that was a county seat had a courthouse where a marriage license could be purchased for $1.75. It seemed to be a very friendly place. The county clerk only asked their ages and believed (or pretended to believe) Amanda was eighteen years old. They signed the application, listened to and repeated the vows, and were through in fifteen minutes. Amanda was dumbfounded. She felt the same and wondered how the $1.75 piece of paper, repeating some jumbled words, and saying "I do" could change her life so drastically, as she knew it had. She would never go back to the little prairie house that was the only home she remembered. It appeared she would, evidently, live in Mr. C.'s big house on Mabrey Street.

On the way back to Northeast Texas, Mr. C. tried to explain to Amanda why the economy was stagnant and the want and poverty was so widespread. "At one time," he said, "I read that America had lost more lives in the first four years of the nationwide Depression than during the World War."

Amanda had read what she could find about what was going on here, but she failed to comprehend the magnitude of the needy and why the people in power could watch it happen and do nothing about it.

Mr. C. said, "A lot of banks have failed, and some bankers and moneyed people, having lost everything, have committed suicide. They would rather die than live in failure. Other banks have a strict policy to foreclose on any note that is not being paid. That is what I am trying to change as fast as I possibly can."

"But you are on the Bank Board. Can't you insist the bank must give some leeway to those with families?"

"I am glad you brought that up. That is my one-man crusade. I don't have controlling interest in the bank stock right now, but I am slowly getting there. I have a list of shareholders who will vote with me, and I am, one at a time, paying off banknotes with bank shares as collateral."

"Does Mr. Carter, the bank president, know what you are doing?" And Amanda looked at her new husband with a new regard.

"Maybe he is beginning to suspect it. So far, he hasn't mentioned it to me, and I think he knows when he does, I will tell him and the whole board of directors we must do something for the ones in real need and not quite ready to go on relief."

"What is 'relief?' And how does it work? I have heard my daddy scream and cry that my mother and I are trying to put him on 're-lief"! That was when we asked for some things that were absolute necessities…" Amanda's voice quivered and finally faded away.

"Yes, J. M. would feel that way, for in a convoluted way, he is proud. That is one of the reasons he is not able to accept what he considers are your mistakes at this time."

She said, "I know. His whole attitude is that I am trying to disgrace him…but…how are we going to help people who are losing everything and don't have collateral for a loan or something we can buy? The store is not making…" She stopped and looked so guilty that Mr. C. laughed and said,

"I know you do enough checking up and banking that you realize the store is carrying way too many charge accounts on the books, and we need to do something about them. But I don't need a lot of money. If you will notice, most of the charge accounts that are far behind are families with babies or small children and/or sickness in the family. That was what started me paying off banknotes with bank shares for security for some folks."

He looked troubled and said, "One day old Cap Jones came in the store, and I could tell he had something on his mind. He was nervous as a call girl in church…" He stopped and looked ashamed of having used an off-color expression. Amanda grinned and he continued. "When all the customers were gone, I turned and waited because I knew he had something on his mind that was bothering him. He stomped around, chewed up a match stem,, and tried to swallow something that tasted bad…bitter like gall.

"'Well,' he said, 'You know with my stock and a stock trailer, I've been picking up livestock for the bank when it forecloses on them.'"I said, 'Yes, I heard that.'"Well,' Cap said, 'that son of a'—well, you know what he said." He had choked on the last word, and Amanda laughed. "'That Carter called me to go out to Matt Williams's place and pick up his last cow.' He stumbled around like he was ashamed to show the emotion tearing him apart. 'Those people have a baby.' He was choking. 'I told my wife last night I wasn't going to do it, and you know what she said? Oh yes you are. Somebody is going to haul that cow, and it's going to be you. We need the money to see us through this. We have to take care of our own kids.'"Then Old Cap, who everybody knows is a bootlegger and a woman chaser, broke down and cried like a baby." Mr. C. waited a bit, and then he said, "This Depression is really something. It has made some pretty good men bad, but it has also made some pretty bad men good. One thing it's done is making us all realize life can be changed and times can be hard without our having any say-so in it. But one thing we have to decide is, which side are we going to be on?"

The big car purred through the countryside, and both its occupants were quiet, and it seemed as if their moods were mellow and a little companionable. The leaves on the sides of the road were a solid artwork, and the sunshine was just right to help them glitter and shine. The fog of the morning had made this road seem an eerie sort of place. Now it was gone, and the brilliance of the reds and golds was breathtaking. Amanda felt something wonderful had happened in her life, something that was finally good. There was someone who believed in her. Someone who understood her, or if he did not, he would at least listen to her pleas for understanding. That was something she had always craved…but had never had.

Chapter 2

When the couple drove into town, they did not stop at the store. They passed through the town square and turned south at the intersection toward Mr. C.'s home. When they were stopped in the garage, Amanda felt a quiver of uneasiness that caused her throat to close up and her legs to shake as she left the warm, friendly automobile. What was she going to do? This was the home of a very prominent businessman. How could she live here—be the wife of a town leader who was very respected, was on boards, an elder of his church and an alderman of the town?

Could she live in his home and take over more of his business, as he had asked her to? Could she be a wife to him and a helpmate? Could she do what he needed her to and look the town people in the eye with a clear mind and conscience? She really did not know, but she had promised herself and the Lord, while she had mumbled the vows, she would do everything in her power to be what he needed.

She knew this man was the finest, most trustworthy man she had ever known, and she loved and respected him with an emotion that had nothing to do with romance; it was a feeling she had never had before. One her parents had never seemed to entertain toward each other or to her, and she had never found it anywhere, hidden in mind and heart. It was as if the feeling were a tiny little shoot, a soft, whitish green that maybe would take root and grow, and she felt she might know what it was. Could it possibly be a sprouted seed of… what? Could it be love? Something kind and soft and beautiful? She hoped so…oh, how she hoped so. And she hoped it would grow and multiply and fill up her life…and her heart, because her heart was empty, dried up and…what was the word she needed? A desert, her heart was a desert.

When Mr. C. opened the door to the house, his longtime cook and housekeeper met them, and Amanda could see the disbelief and shock on the lady's face.

"Mrs. Barrett, this is Amanda Connor, my wife. I know you have met her before, but not as my wife, and I know you will treat her with respect as lady of this house. If you want to, you can continue on as housekeeper and cook, with the grocery listing and meal planning. If you choose not to, there will be no hard feelings. Bubba will still be errand boy and garden and yard keeper. I know he and Amanda are compatible, as she knows and understands him from their work at the store."

Mrs. Barrett was so shocked and speechless it was almost comical to watch her try to take control of her expression and find her voice. Her eyes were chasing each other around and refused to alight on Amanda or Mr. C. She nodded her head and turned to go into the kitchen, and then Amanda saw Bubba go to the table and pick up a place setting. Then Mr. C. stood very still and waited for something. He asked Mrs. Garrett if she had cooked the meal he had asked for before he left that morning. She nodded, but Amanda could see she still felt this was not real. Amanda could sympathize with her on that, because she still felt this whole day was unreal and maybe impossible.

Mr. C. said as they stopped in the kitchen doorway, "You see, Mrs. Barrett, Amanda will be working with me at the store most of the time, and I can't expect her to be full-time there and contend with three meals a day, the laundry, and the care of the household. With an extra person living here, if you think all this will be too much for you, we can hire you some part time help or maybe a housecleaning person to come in one day a week. It is up to you... We'll see how it goes."

Mrs. Barrett nodded, and with that seemingly off his mind, Mr. C. said, "Amanda, we need to go upstairs, and you can choose which room you want." This was said in a very matter-of-fact tone, and she looked at him once, straightened her shoulders, and followed him up the wide, curving stairway. To her consternation, she realized this was to be an in-name-only marriage and felt it might be better that way. She knew absolutely nothing about marriage except what she had read, and the only thing she knew for sure about it was that she would never, never marry if her life would be spent as her mother's was.

In a way she felt sad this wonderful man was to live out his life with a silly little ignorant girl who had never been anywhere, had no education, and was too young and naive to be a real wife to him. "Well," she thought, "I am going to be the very best help I can be, and I hope he is never sorry he has done what he has this day."

The bed in the room she picked out was going to be a great place to sleep. In fact, she loved the whole room, especially the bedside tables with lamps on them. That was one of the things that had made her feel cheated while she was growing up. They had not had electricity. By the time she had finished all her chores, her dad was ready for bed and had insisted the lamps must be turned out.

The first meal Amanda ate in her new home was pleasant as far as her new husband was concerned, but she felt a stiffness coming from the kitchen. She noticed a questioning glance from Bubba as he sat at the kitchen table in sight of her in the dining room. He was puzzled about something, she knew, because he only looked that way when he did not understand what was going on. She finished her meal and asked Mr. C. if he was ready to rest, and he agreed. Then she picked up their plates and silverware and carried them to the kitchen sink. Mrs. Barrett gave her a look that was not resentful, but she got the feeling she was doing something in somebody else's territory.

With that done, she went to her room, curled up on her bed, and tried to think. Then there was a tap on her door, and she flew from the bed. When she said "Come in," Mr. C entered the room. She still felt she was in the fetal position, even in the chair, but she hoped he would not see her depressed and with the helpless feeling that had started when they had entered the house.

He sat on the chest at the foot of the bed and said, "Amanda, I know this is all strange to you and will seem that way for a little while, but it will work out. We just need a little time. I hope you will give people a chance to know you, and try to understand, if you can, we have set things up for a real shocker." He grinned, and she wondered how he could seem so relaxed and pleased, knowing what happened with Mrs. Barrett was going to go on for a long time with the people of this town.

Then he said, "Good night, Amanda. If you need anything, let me or Mrs. Barrett know. She and Bubba go to their house as soon as they finish in the kitchen." He stood as though he wanted to say more, but then he said, "Good night again." And went to his room. She heard the Barretts go home soon after and took an account of what had happened to her, and said a little prayer that asked if she could be guided in the situation she found herself in now. She realized she needed help now and would through the years ahead.

The next day after the marriage, Amanda awoke with a sense of well-being, and she felt she could do anything she set her heart and mind to. Mr. C. was dressed and downstairs when she followed the odors of cooking food to the kitchen. When she got to the dining room, she apologized for being tardy, and Mr. C. shrugged his shoulders and asked why she felt she should get up early.

"Well, I really don't know. Maybe we had better wait and see."

"Would you be terribly unhappy not going to school right now?"

Amanda studied a bit and finally said, "I really don't know. Maybe if I can work with you full-time, that would be better and mean more than working part-time, as I was doing. There is so much about the business I want to learn, and I can read and study. I can write well enough, and you know I can figure and make change. Maybe studying and working with you will be enough for right now."

"Then let's get on up there and see how Thomas did yesterday." He turned toward the kitchen door and said to Mrs. Barrett, "We won't be home for lunch today, as we are going to be in and out of the store, but how about fried chicken for supper?" If Mrs. Barrett answered him, it did not come through to Amanda's ears, and she wondered if she and that lady were going to make do with their situation or if there was trouble brewing. She knew she would do her very best to make life as easy as she possibly could for Mr. C., but there was a limit for things. She had felt shock and real animosity last night at mealtime, and if that was the way the lady felt, that was her problem. Yet if it came to ugliness, she would not be treated as she had been all her life. This was a new life, and she wanted it to be better than what she had in her old life. If the shock and astonishment she felt would come from everyone, she would find it hard to survive, yet she would not be walked on, especially by other employees. She must start out as she could hold out.

The town wireless news was in full swing when they got to town. It seemed easy for Mr. C. to say, "Yes, it is true, Amanda and I are married, and yes, we are going to continue to run the store, except we will run it as a fifty-fifty partnership. Her name will be on the store and the checkbook. Yes, she may go to market, and maybe she will want to handle some material, notions, and ladies' wear."

In a while Mr. C. left to go to the lawyer's office after Thomas McGraed came in to help at the store. She and Thomas fell back into the rhythm they had worked out last summer. The questions being asked of her now that Mr. C. was not there could have been staggering had she faltered in her answers. She took her cue from his attitude. By the time Mr. C. came back to the store, Amanda was in a daze, switching back and forth from comedy to outright rage and fear. Mr. C. was his relaxed, genteel self and seemed happy about the way things were going.

He suggested they go across to Minningers and have a bite to eat. She wondered why he was subjecting them to more public scrutiny, but she saw he was saying, "This is my wife; please accept her." Amanda found she loved and respected him more as she watched him cope with the questions of the many people who seemed to not only to find out they were married but also believed they knew why. A few times, when she was out of Mr. C.'s hearing, some nosy female simpered and snickered and outright asked her how she got him to marry her. Judy Cagel made the remark that everybody would know in nine months. Hee-hee-hee.

By the end of the day, Amanda was a nervous wreck and was so angry she could not eat the fried chicken and gravy Mrs. Barrett had cooked. It looked and smelled delicious, and she knew she needed food in her stomach, but she found it hard to swallow. The problem was, her stomach was sending the message that the food might come back up with burning, bitter bile.

When the meal was over, Amanda excused herself and went to her room, climbed on her bed, and tried to make some kind of order in her whirling brain. In a while, Mr. C. knocked and waited for her to tell him to come in. She wondered how in the world she could spare this wonderful man the agony of admitting he had made a mistake. She could see it had been a mistake and thought she should be the one to acknowledge it.

Mr. C. sat on the chest at the end of the bed again and held a hand up to sign her to wait to talk. He ran his hands down both sides of his face, smiled, and said, "Amanda, I knew you could do this. I am so proud of the way you handled yourself today, and I believe today was the worst of it. They will all settle down and get used to our being here and seeing you are a good and honest person, and I am lucky to have you."

"But Mr. C., they believe I tricked you into marrying me. How can they believe that? I have never done any of them harm or acted in a sleazy way."

He looked at her with understanding and was very solemn. Then he said, "I hate to say this because you never should have to learn it at such a young age. Most of the people who are so suspicious of others, and believe the very worst of them, are usually the people whom they, themselves, have never measured up. I find it hard to trust those who are so eager to believe the very worst of others. As I said, I'm sorry they have been so unkind today, but it is going to work, and as I said, I am so proud of you. I knew you could handle it. And you did." He gave her a beaming, lovely smile and said, "Good night, Amanda. If you feel this is too much for you, stay home a bit; rearrange the house; go to Greenville and shop."

She said what she really and truly believed with all her heart. "I enjoy being with you, and I want to work with you. I want to live here with you. I want you to teach me all I am capable of learning. Will you do that?"

"I will, and feel honored you feel this way." So saying, he left her to go to his own bedroom. Then it dawned on her she had said she wanted to live with him. Her face burned with embarrassment, and she wondered what he had thought of her remark, if the words had a connotation other than what she had meant. She wondered if he thought she was a low-class person who wanted to be in his bed...in any man's bed. She wondered if he could ever want her as his real wife.

In her mind, she mulled over how kind and gracious was this wonderful man who had married her. He had given her a home that was far beyond any hopes she had ever dreamed possible. When she had daydreamed and fantasized about a home she would love to have when she grew up and married, it had never been so wonderful as this one.

Mr. C. was right. The first day they had gone to the store after their marriage was the worst day they had. The people settled down and came mostly to the store to trade. They were curious, but not openly so, and only asked questions that made sense. The schoolkids who came into the store seemed to be curious, as if they would like to ask embarrassing questions, but none of them did.

Amanda became a little surer of her ability to cope with the workings of the business and dealings with the customers. Some of them asked some slightly obtuse questions, and she felt they might want to see her in error, so she became very sure of her answers.

The noon hour they spent in the store, she with a peanut-butter-and-banana sandwich and Mr. C. with cheese and crackers and a tin of sardines. He apologized for the smell of the sardines, but he had a little smile on his face that captured her imagination as well as her attention.

Then, when a customer came in the front door while they were eating, Mr. C. went up front to wait on him, and finally Amanda heard him say, "Yes, sardines do smell up the place, but Amanda really does love them. So we look over that." Amanda listened to him tell such a blatant fib and wondered how such a fine, spiritual man could do such a thing.

When he came back to the little pockmarked table, his look reminded her of a kid caught with a hand in a cookie jar. She gave him a severe look and said, "Boy, are you in trouble!"

With an unrepentant look, he said, "I couldn't remember which one of us wanted the sardines." Then he took the empty can out the back door and put it in the trash barrel. At that time, Amanda realized her time with this man would never be boring.

Days began to pass fast; Amanda became engrossed in the workings of the store and was making a self-absorbing effort to make some progress every day with the running of the business. The county library was across the street. For the first time in her life, she signed for a card and began hunting for books she felt would help her in her quest for the knowledge of business and government. She studied the three branches of the national government and tried to understand why the stock market had collapsed and money had become almost nonexistent.

She had only seen her father one time since she had left home, and when she saw him at the front, she had gone through the back door. For some reason she was not afraid of him anymore and could have faced him, but she thought it would be better if she did not…yet. She knew Mr. C. had talked to him the day she had tried to go home and thought they might have talked since then. She hoped maybe they would see each other someday and be able to speak to each other, but not yet. She felt she would weep, and that was too immature and childlike to consider. She needed to have more control over her feelings when she looked him in the eye and spoke to him.

He had looked solemn and gaunt, and he had lost his quick, purposeful steps and mannerisms. In fact, he had entered hesitantly, and she could not put this person she was seeing today in the place of the J. M. Mason that, in her growing years, she had feared.

Mr. C. had seen her leave through the back door and had waited until they were on the way home to ask if she thought the time would come when she could see her dad and talk to him. When she told him she thought so, hoped so, he had said, "When you feel you are ready, just tell me."

After a few days, she did not cry anymore, and the few times she did, it was in bed, after supper, in her room. She would not upset or worry Mr. C. after he had retired for the night. Most of the time, her problem had been because of something Mrs. Barrett had done or said, or something she had not said. She felt the lady had made a few little innuendoes, even some sly little looks that would be hard to make a big deal over. Once, she had thought to set the table, but when they had sat to eat, the silverware had been placed on the edge of the plates rather than beside them, where she had laid them.

Some of the time, she felt maybe she should take a stand, but mostly she blamed her nerves being on edge and the fact that she was exhausted from the tension that built at the store. She did not feel the housekeeper was trying to be hateful. She knew Mrs. Barrett had run the household for a long time, even when Mrs. Leona was still alive. Maybe she just wanted to be sure the running of it was still hers, and she wanted no competition.

Most of the time when Mrs. Barrett rubbed her the wrong way, Amanda knew any unpleasantness would put more strain on Mr. C., and she felt he was exhausted from the full days he was spending at the store.

When the first week had passed and Saturday closing time came, Amanda drew a sigh of relief and thought maybe she would stay in bed tomorrow and rest both Saturday and Sunday nights. Her mind was exhausted, and though her body was used to physical labor, it was not used to the strain of being in the right place at the right time and making sure everything she did was right and proper.

When the locks were on the doors and Amanda started toward the car, Mr. C. looked at her and said, "I know you are tired, but

Mrs. Albany said she would stay a little late and let you try on a dress or two for church on Sundays. Do you thank you could?"

For just a minute, Amanda thought she was going to fall apart. Then she took one look at his face and his very hopeful expression, straightened her shoulders, and said she thought so. Then she saw a whole new man. Her dear Mr. C. had control of her life, and she could not begin to count the ways he was changing her future. She was also changing his life and lifestyle almost as much as he was changing hers. If she was to go to church with him, of course she needed something decent to wear. He had seen the old navy blue dress she had worn to Oklahoma, and certainly he had known that was all she had.

When they entered the dress shop, Mrs. Albany had laid out two dresses she thought would do for Amanda to wear to church and on other dressy occasions. Amanda took them to the dressing room and put on the deep forest green one. When she turned to the mirror and saw herself, she almost gasped out loud. Color rushed to her face, and she smiled at the jaunty girl who looked back at her. She could not stop looking. She had never seen herself in a dress that showed her tiny waistline and cradled her breasts. She had never known a shade of rich and shimmery green could brighten her complexion and make her eyes glimmer and glisten. She stood entranced and so stunned she could not move.

Mr. C. finally called her name, and she cleared the frog from her throat and said "Coming" in a very small voice.

When she stepped out into the store, there was an offset in the wall with three mirrors in it, and she could see herself from all angles. When she looked, Mrs. Albany nodded her head in satisfaction, and when she looked at Mr. C., he was beaming. When she could find her voice again, she said, "Isn't it terribly expensive?"

Mrs. Albany hurried to say, "No, not really, and it will wear in all seasons." And her husband—and she was beginning to feel she belonged to him—was smiling and appeared happy.

He said, "It is beautiful and worth every dime."

She tried the other dress on, which was a rich chocolate brown in a long-wearing faille. It was a perfect fit too. Mrs. Albany brought out a pair of silk stockings and said, "C. J. says you have some pumps that will go well with these dresses, and anyway, it will be a while before Mallory's will get any new shoes. You don't need to wear shoes that everybody has a pair just like them, anyway." And then she smiled at Amanda as if they had a secret. She put the hose and some frilly underwear into a smaller bag, being sure Amanda saw them, then put that bag into the one with the dresses.

With Mr. C. carrying the packages, they left the store, strolled toward the car and went to the house…not just to the house…but *home.* That wonderful thought came to her so suddenly, and she wanted this wonderful man to know how she felt. It surely seemed that if she could have daydreamed and fantasized about a home to have someday, it would never have been as lovely and grand as the one they lived in now.

She had been here before they married, bringing keys and other things to him, but she had not been inside until the night of their wedding.

The house was not old. It had been built soon after the turn of the century, but it was in a gracious plantation style with big white columns in front and tall windows. The porches wrapped two sides of the house, and on the front, there was another porch on the second floor, which was actually the roof of the lower porch.

On the second floor, the windows of the front two bedrooms opened onto that porch, or deck, and from her window, there was a view to be checked out when she had time. She wondered if it would be safe to venture out there, and how would the town look from up there?

She said to herself she had all the time in the world to look and explore. Mr. C. had told her when he got back from the lawyer's office the first day that the home was hers…even in her name. A shiver ran along her arm, and another ran up her spine when she thought of living here without him. He had insisted they not talk of the ifs of the future, of what was going to happen; they were just to live each day as it came.

He said he had the business part of his will rewritten to the best of his ability and hoped she would have no trouble when the time came when she would have to do everything herself. He said all this in a rational, straightforward manner, and she listened in silence. She tried not to betray her sadness and fear when he talked about this, for the thought of his leaving made her heart ache and her mind refuse to function.

He said the bank business was in a fireproof box with the list of folks with banknotes who still owned some bank stock. "The stock is next to worthless right now, but it will recover when the economy does, and we need control of 51 percent of the shares to be able to change things. The lockbox is here, as I have not thought leaving it at the bank was a good idea. Too many people have access to things at the bank, and anyway, the people who owe the bank and still have bank shares are proud and want to believe we are not giving them charity."

The saving of other people's feelings appeared to matter to him a great deal. Amanda wished with all her heart he did not have to worry about so many others' feelings during his recuperation after the heart attack.

The she said, "Mr. C. you have given me too much already. I am not smart enough, old enough, or brave enough to tend to this business of yours without you to guide me. Please find someone you can trust to do the things I will never be able to do." And she wept.

"Amanda, you will not be alone in this. The Halseys, my lawyers, have been involved from the beginning. They will never leave you stranded, wondering what to do and how to do it. They will never make your decisions for you, but they will help you decide how to do what needs to be done. All right?"

Since Mr. C. had promised things were going to be better and the people had settled down, she did not feel now they were actors in a sideshow. She began to work hard and steadily. She also started to feel at home in this new life. She found herself living in a set pattern and a feeling of finding her place. The people came into the store mostly to shop now, not to find out about Mr. Connor and his new young wife. Amanda never mentioned school. The few students who came into the store looked eager to ask question but never seemed to get the courage to make any conversations. She became a little surer of herself and her ability to cope with the workings of the business and called less and less for Mr. C.'s attention. Some customers asked some rather obtuse questions, leading her to believe, in a way, they were looking and waiting for her to make an error, so she became very careful and sure of her answers before she gave a definite opinion.

The noon hour was spent, most of the time, in the store, at the little pockmarked table in the back. Mr. C. often had slices of cheese and the ever-ready tin of sardines. Amanda usually made herself a peanut-butter-and-banana sandwich, which she loved, along with her favorite soda water in the grape flavor. Mr. C. always apologized for the smell of the sardines, but he always had the quirky little smile on his face, and it always captured her imagination. The lunchtime was a welcome break in their workdays. She laughed a lot, and he always managed to please her with his funny little sayings and ditties. They slipped into the habit of saying things that were interesting out of the range of the business. She asked questions that brought about conversations whereby Amanda could pick up little bits of knowledge—little kernels of wisdom from this very wise man that she carefully filed away in her mind to use in the future. While they ate, he always seemed to drop his business mien and became a down to earth everyday fellow—a clown who did the turkey trot and asked all sorts of riddles. He did all this, she knew, just to hear her laugh.

One day she asked, "Why do you always break me up like this?"

And he said, "Amanda, you don't know how great it is for me to hear you laugh. The first time I ever heard you really laugh was the first day I ate the sardines. That was a wonderful sound to me. I know you were not taught to laugh, but please, please, do it a lot. It is good for your soul and very, very good for my soul too. When you first came to work here, your experience of finding fun in sayings was absolutely nonexistent. I could not believe that when I pulled an inanity, you just stood there and waited to find some sense in what I said. There was no sense in it—just a little bit of wit, and you had not been introduced to wit. I think that was terribly sad."

The little grin was back on his face, which made him look the proverbial boy with his hand in the jar again. She promised herself that her job was to make his life easier and, by all means, more pleasant. If spouting nonsense was the way to do it, then she would make *him* smile a lot.

From that day on, when he opened the tin of sardines, he got the grin in place, and she tried to find new ways to be outlandishly repulsed by the odor and to be a picture of their very priggish Mrs. Cheney, who still lived in the Olde British World where she had been reared. Amanda usually held her nose and acted offended and very prim until the sardine can was dutifully stowed into the trash barrel outside. Once, she even stuck a clothespin onto her nose. She laughed mostly because she felt free of fear, tension, and dread. She realized her time with her husband was to be a joyous, happy time, and she vowed to love every minute of it. She knew Mr. C. believed in harmony and relaxation and expected her to enjoy every day, to find goodness and to see humor in every situation. The whole concept of life as he lived it was so new and strange to her she barely believed in it. But she embraced it wholeheartedly.

The Mr. C. said, "Since we have found how wonderful it is to hear you laugh, will you make a habit of it, Amanda?"

And she said, "How could I not laugh with a clown like you around?"

Chapter 3

Days began to pass swiftly as Amanda became engrossed in the workings of the business of the store. An interest she had in mind, aside from the math, was history and government. She studied the three branches of the federal government and tried to understand how it could work. She knew that America was a very young nation; it was so new that this was still in a trial period. This Depression was a faltering step, even more so than the World War. In fact, she felt it was the worst thing to befall the young nation, with the exception of the War Between the States. She was very concerned another division could happen, and might be fatal to the nation. The War Between the States had proved unity was essential for survival, and she felt, in some very positive way, the gap between the haves and the have-nots must be closed, at least part of the way. Her schoolbooks taught there were only a handful of millionaires in America today.

She prayed for the hungry, the very needy, for herself and this town and community. Most of all, she prayed for her wonderful Mr. C. She made certain he was never left to listen to any unhappy customer, that he rested as his friend Dr. Story had ordered. She tried to see that at bedtime, he left her with no troubles from her or anyone else in the family. She did think of herself, and the Barretts, as his family, and she made sure there was no touch of unpleasantness in anyone's actions at Mr. C.'s table, and afterward, until bedtime—his bedtime, anyway.

She enjoyed her time after supper and remembered to tell the Lord and Mr. C. how she appreciated her wonderful bedside lamps and the freedom to move about and study after he retired. His friend Dr. Story was adamant he had eight hours rest at night and at least one hour in the early afternoon.

Amanda wondered occasionally about her mother. When she had seen her dad that one time, he had looked gaunt and unsure of himself, which was a look diametrically opposed to her longtime opinion of him. His mannerisms were hesitant, and she could not put this, what she had seen of him that day, with the J. M. Mason whom she had grown up around. He had seemed unsure of his role in her life now; therefore, she felt unsure of her own fold in her life with him as her father.

She did not cry much anymore, and when she did, it was when she was tired to exhaustion, one of Mrs. Barrett's oblique questions about the household or Amanda's clothes, or Mrs. Barrett's cooking. It was clear that if Amanda was tired, then Mr. C. was exhausted, and any unpleasantness would be debilitating enough that Mr. C. would rest very little that night. He needed a calm rest, so Amanda turned away, went to her wonderful room, her many books, and shut out her failure to be a friend to Mrs. Barrett. Bubba was easy to be with at the store and around the house, so she knew the block between herself and housekeeper was not all her fault. Mr. C. had asked her to handle all of these things without denial and emotional upheaval, and she tried.

She felt that when she had built daydreams of her home of the future, she had never pictured it to be so lovely as her wonderful home she loved, here, with all her heart. She did not have the time to work, to study, to enjoy her life and work those hours with Mr. C. without Mrs. Barrett here to do the house and meals. So Amanda began to figure ways to let Mrs. Barrett know she was appreciated. That was the point when she asked why Mrs. Barrett and Bubba could not eat with them as a family. She remembered Bubba had hesitantly picked up a third plate from the dining table the night of their wedding and their trip to Oklahoma. She now believed it was a little silly for four people to eat at separate tables, and when she said so, Mr. C. agreed. So they ate their night meal together, and Amanda did not help clear the table or offer to do the dishes. She knew Mrs. Barrett felt it was her job to finish the housework before she and Bubba left to cross the garden patch to their home.

Amanda and Mr. C. talked some in the living room at night, especially as the weather turned cool enough for a fire in the fireplace. She felt it was a very homey and pleasant place to be, and the fire was there more for pleasure than warmth, as there were gas heaters for taking the chill from the rooms of the house.

He mentioned again the bank business in a fireproof box with a list of folks with banknotes who still owned some bank shares. "The stock is practically worthless right now, but it will recover as the economy does, and we need 51 percent of the stock if we are to change anything. The box is here, as I have not thought leaving it at the bank was a good idea. Too many people have access to things at the bank. And besides," he said, "some of the people we are helping are proud and believe we are not giving them charity and advertising it." Twice he told her these things, and his ideas to save the feelings of others seemed to matter a lot. Amanda wished he did not have to worry about others so much during the recuperation from his heart attack.

Then Amanda said, "Mr. C., you have given me too much already. Let me say again I am not smart enough, old enough, or brave enough to tend to this business without you to guide me. Please stay with me until I am grown up enough, mature enough, to do it; or if you can't stay, find somebody you trust to do the things I'll not be able to do." And again, in spite of all that she could do, she wept.

"Amanda, you will not be alone with no one to guide you. You know my lawyers, Hap and John Halsey; you can trust them. They will never leave you wondering what to do and how to do it. They have been in on everything I've done so far, and you will have the same help that I've had. All right?" And she did believe maybe things would be close to all right.

The next morning, after the first week of her marriage, she combed and dressed her hair to the best of her ability. It was heavy, shoulder-length brown with auburn highlights. She decided to wear the chocolate-brown dress first. She felt going to Mr. C.'s church for the first time in something so outstanding as the beautiful green frock might be misconstrued as flaunting clothes finer than she had ever had before.

When she got downstairs, Mr. C. was dressed and at the table, drinking coffee and reading the paper. He looked up as she neared the table and said, "Amanda, you look very nice."

Her throat felt as if there were a baseball stuck in it. There was a little time before she could say, "So do you, Mr. C.," and he did. He was wearing a three-piece brown suit with a white shirt and a diagonally striped brown-and-gold tie. He was freshly shaved, and his shock of blond-and-gray hair was combed and parted. She wondered how she was going to walk beside him into that beautiful brick church building with everybody looking at them. She was still wondering why and how she was married to this fine man.

She found later it was easier to be escorted by him than she thought it would be. Mr. C. looked at the people with whom he shared this church and spoke to them with an open countenance as he ushered her down the aisle. Amanda could see no uneasiness or question in his manner, voice, or walk. He treated her with the same respect he dealt with other ladies in business and socially. He chose the pew they were to sit in by a touch of his hand on her elbow and a nod of his head. He waited for her to be seated before he sat beside her. He did not sit close to her, but not far away either.

She knew her face was flushed, and she was unsure of herself, but she soon became engrossed in the rituals of this church's worship hour. The order was somewhat different from that of her church in the country, but she still felt the church was here to be used as a place to sing praises, read scriptures, and pray. What else was needed? When the service was over, many folks came to speak to them and left the impression that, as their respected member was her sponsor, she was accepted. She was handed a Sunday school tract and invited to come in time for the Sunday school hour.

With a sigh of relief, she felt wonderful as they walked into their house and was proud to be here in their wonderful home. She really did feel at home here, even more so, it seemed, without Mrs. Barrett in the kitchen.

When she asked Mr. C. what he wanted her to fix for their lunch, he said Mrs. Barrett usually left him a meat dish, a vegetable or two, and a dessert of sorts. These things they found, so Amanda set the table with napkins, silverware, plates, and glasses. Setting the table was an easy chore for her, as her mother had her do that most of the time at home. She wondered shakily what this dear man would think when he found she had never cooked a meal in her life. He had gone to the stove and was emptying bowls of food into pans, and burners under the pans were lighting like magic with a twist of a handle. He stirred the food in the pans and let them heat as he took ice from the refrigerator and put it in glasses she brought from the table. Then she added tea from a pitcher that was in the bottom of the refrigerator.

At home they had ice very seldom after the Model A car quit running, because the ice melted faster than a horse could travel the miles home, even when it was wrapped in paper and in a gunnysack. They had lowered milk into the well each morning in hot weather to keep if from souring, and food was cooked only when it would soon be eaten.

This house, this home, was a magic place, and she did not know why all this was happening to her. She was much too ignorant— well, if not ignorant, she was a green country girl, just as Boyd Chalmers had said, and felt completely out of her depth. She tried to tell Mr. C. how it was all unreal and she was not good enough or smart enough to deserve the blessings that kept happening to her.

Mr. C. looked at her and said, "What makes you think I am smart enough and good enough to merit the blessings that have come to me in my lifetime? We must be grateful, but we must not question all the gifts from the Father." They sat to enjoy their meal, and it was a while before Amanda took up more of her thoughts and expressed them:

"But Mr. C., you are smart and good; you do wonderful things in your church and the town, and everybody knows it. They all love and respect you because you are always ready to do what needs to be done. You do what you can for people regardless of who they are, and so... I'll never forget you as long as I live, even if I live to be a hundred! You are my place of peace and safety. There's no telling what would have happened to me if you had not stepped in. I just don't know why you have done so much for me. I was in dire circumstances that day you asked me to work for you. It...it was because you knew I had to have supplies if I was to go to school, and that Daddy would not, or could not, give them to me. I think he thought they were unnecessary." And she stopped talking, as the tears were getting too close to falling, and her throat was clogged up.

"Amanda, I may not have done enough for you to keep trials and troubles away from your future. There may come a time when you may wish I had stayed out of your life; that I had not burdened you with my little plans for the future and for the folks here. You may find, when you take a stand, those men will try to belittle you or dishonor you with greed and ridicule. I just hope you will be strong enough to finish what my little dreams have started." So saying, he left her to go to his room to rest his hour, which Dr. Story insisted on being his habit seven days a week.

* * * * *

On Monday, Mr. C. was on the telephone for a while. When he finished, he came to where Amanda was culling some Irish potatoes and told her Dr. Story could see her in his office now. He said to feel free to freshen up and go on over to the office, and to know Dr. Story was a fine man, a dedicated doctor, and would be very patient and kind to her. Amanda looked at him as if he had lost his mind. Why in the world did he think she needed to see a doctor, and why would he make the appointment without even mentioning it to her? When she asked him those questions, he seemed taken aback and asked her why she had a problem with this.

She said, "I have never been in a doctor's office in my life, and I don't think I need one now. Do you?"

Finally, he said, "I want the best care possible for you. Would you just do this for me? It is just a physical and won't take long, and it will settle my mind."

And of course, she agreed because she did not want him to worry about anything, especially about her. He seemed relieved when she had washed up and was ready to go, and she did see the stand she had taken against him had bothered him. His face was flushed, and he seemed a little more worried than she had seen him before.

At Dr. Story's office, she sat on a chair and waited for him to call her. She almost giggled, thinking this was called a waiting room because this was where one waited. When the doctor stuck his head around the doorway and said, "Amanda Connor," she knew she had not waited long enough. She wanted to take to her heels and run, but she answered, "Yes."

He asked her to come into the inner office and told her to be seated on the end of a table. Dr. Story told her he had asked Mr. C. H. to come over with her, but her husband had thought it was not necessary. He said, "I know you are young and inexperienced, and this may seem awkward to you, but I will be as gentle as I can be." Then he picked up the blood pressure cuff (which she had read about), folded it around her arm, pumped it up, and seemed to be counting. Then he checked her eyes, nose, and ears, had her open her mouth, and used a tongue depressor to look in her throat. That gagged her. When he put the gadgets back in his ears and pushed a cold object against her chest, right above her breast, she almost came unwound. He saw it, for he said, "Easy, Amanda, I'm not going to do anything that isn't necessary."

When he turned aside and started washing his hands, he asked her to take off her panties and to lie back on the table, and she almost choked to death. She had felt a little better when he had done the blood pressure thing and listened to her chest, but now she was mortified. This was awful, and she said, "Do I have to do this?" And the doctor looked at her with the kindest eyes she had ever seen and said, "Yes, it is very necessary." To her he seemed almost as nervous as she was.

Then he asked her to scoot backward on the table. He picked up her right foot, bent her leg at the knee, and put her foot firmly in a stirrup-type contraption. She became really alarmed and said, "I am scared out of my wits, so let's forget this whole thing and let me leave, *now*!"

Then he said, "Amanda, you know I would not hurt you for the world. And...I wouldn't do this if it didn't need to be done."

So she gritted her teeth and felt like some animal, a pig, maybe, she had seen strung up, ready to be scraped or maybe...gutted? She clenched her teeth; they were still chattering, and she tried to shut out what was going on down at her lower body. She felt something cold at the entrance of her body, and something entered there. Then she heard a noise, like a shocked grunt, from her doctor. Then he took her feet from the stirrups, placed his hand under her shoulder, and said, "Upsy-daisy." Then he went to the lavatory and washed his hands for a long, long time.

She slipped her panties back on and knew her lower body part had grease on it, maybe petroleum jelly? When she glanced up, Dr. Story's face was as red as hers, and he had trouble looking at her. He sat behind his desk and tried to be calm as he finished the examination by asking her questions about her monthly periods and others she felt he had no business knowing. Then she asked if she could go now, and when he said "yes," she left as fast as she could and promised herself she would never be caught in a doctor's office again. She could spit on the man who had embarrassed her and the one who had made her come over to him. How much more could she take in this crazy world she had found herself in?

Doctors seemed to want to know everything about a woman, or why else would he ask her all those crazy questions about her periods and seem shocked at her answers? When she had left the office, he had seemed puzzled about something, worried, and at a loss. She became frantic about what he had found in the examination. What was so horrible about her body the man could not look at her? Was she deformed? Or so ugly he couldn't talk about it or look her in the face?

She was so depressed she could barely weigh Mrs. Cagel's potatoes and bananas. When that was done, she slipped into the bathroom and locked the door. There was something else she had to think about. Maybe she had a terrible disease. Maybe Mr. C. had seen signs of it, and that was why he had sent her over, so the doctor could find out about it for sure.

She heard the phone ring and listened to see if he answered it. In a bit, she heard him call her name, and she raised her voice to tell him she would be out in a minute. Then she heard the front door close.

How was she going to stay here with him if it was as bad as the doctor thought it was? She had always thought she was normal. She had never talked to her mother about her body, especially her lower parts. When she started her periods, her mother had taught her to wear protection pads they made from old sheets. Then her mother had told her a nice girl never let boys hug and kiss her or feel of her, because that made Satan work in boys and men to bring shame to girls. If the girls allowed those liberties, then the boys believed the girl was easy and wanted to be led astray.

She thought she knew what was "led astray." After her bout with the town crowd, she felt sure they, the bunch, all knew about the sex act, and wondered how the girls kept from getting pregnant. Evidently, the little Manning girl had gotten pregnant, and that was what Howard had meant when he said there might be a baby out there who looked like him (Boyd). Boyd had said there might be twins or triplets who looked like all the boys.

"Oh, dear God, that's what they had planned for me!"

She became sick just thinking about it again. If they had caught her, she would have been taken by force, and maybe Mr. C. had thought they had, and she might be pregnant. If he had thought so, why had he not asked?

As time passed and Mr. C. was gone so long, she became completely at sea and thought of a lot of things the doctor could have found wrong with her. Then it dawned on her that regardless of whatever else Dr. Story had found, there was no way she could be pregnant. Had it not been for Howard's help and her key to the store, she might very well be able to have been in that kind of trouble. That was when she knew that when Mr. C. had asked her if she was in *trouble*, that was what he had meant. And that was when she wept.

She became so nervous and shaky she was incapable of running the cash register and getting the money into the bank bag. The tears would not stop, and she became deathly ill.

When Mr. C. came through the door, he asked if she was ready to call it a day. He seemed his old jaunty self, and even though she trembled, and her voice would not work, she began to believe maybe things were not as bad as she had imagined. He seemed to sense how undone and tense she was. He took hold of her arms, looked down into her lovely, swimming eyes, and said, "One question, Amanda. When I asked you, 'Are you in trouble?' what did you think I meant?"

His face was as open and warm as it always was, but there was a light in his eyes that seemed to enter her own. She said, "I thought you meant 'Was I in trouble?' What did you think I meant?

"You had seen my daddy and knew, with his awful temper, I could not possibly go home, or he might kill me. He believed the very worst of me. And my mother had said, 'You are ruined forever.' I had no money and no place to go. This store was the only place I felt safe in the whole world. Boyd Chalmers was out there and had vowed to hunt me down and kill me, or make me pay for getting away from them in his car. I knew I would have been raped and abused—the worst things possible would have happened, because the girls were promising terrible things as well as the boys. What else could I have meant?" Then she crumpled, and he held her while she wept.

Then she raised those bruised, swimming eyes and the dawn of truth hit her harder. She pushed away and said, "Oh God. Oh God! I'm so sorry, Mr. C. You thought I was pregnant! Then you must believe I told you that on purpose. To get you to help me—that I was trying to make my own troubles worse. I'm so sorry! If I could undo all that you've done for me, I would. You must believe I tricked you, but I swear I didn't. I wouldn't. I didn't mean to mislead you. I know, now that everything is out in the open, that you went through all this for nothing." Her breath got caught between her lungs and her throat, and the world spun, and she was choking. Her tears flowed, and he would not turn her loose, and she could not move.

His hands slid up her arms to her shoulders. One big hand rose to cup her chin, and he raised it so she had to look him in the eyes. He ran his finger so very, very gently across her bottom lip and said, "Listen to me, Amanda. This is the greatest news I have had since the Depression hit. You, who I thought had been abused and brutalized, are as pure and healthy as you are supposed to be. I could never see you consenting to sex before marriage, so...I thought it had happened against your will. Can you imagine how it was hurting me to think someone so fine and upstanding had been shamed by what others put you through against your will?"

"Mr. C., I am so sorry this has happened and disrupted your life. Can you make arrangements for me to leave, find a job somewhere, and let you get back to your life, your private life?"

Her eyes were so big and round and so utterly filled with sympathy he chuckled, and then he said,

"Don't be so quick to write me off your list and delegate my poor life to the empty boredom it was before you came into my business and my home. For some reason, I have become attached to my life as it has been the last few weeks." And he chuckled again, and she saw sweetness but no pity in his eyes.

"Are you sure? Do you want to continue on with this…marriage? I think Mrs. Leona would feel bad that little ignorant me is in her beautiful home, sleeping under her lovely handsewn quilts and eating from her beautiful china and silverware. Would she be ashamed I am going with you and sitting in her place in the pew in church, where she used to sit? I can't believe this has happened to me, that you are my legal husband and are asking folks to accept me when I am completely out of your class." And the tears began to fall again, and not only that, but her nose began to run. Once the questions began, they kept coming. She voiced all her doubts and fears she had been mulling over and over in her mind since the day he had offered her marriage and promised her his protection.

He helped her dry her eyes and blow her nose and told her without a doubt, he wanted her in his life and in his home. He asked if she wanted to continue on with their plan, and she surprised him by saying, "Yes, I want to go home…to such a wonderful home… the only place that has ever felt like home to me."

"That, Amanda, is the nicest thing anyone has said to me in a long, long time." When she looked at him, his face was solemn, though maybe a little brighter, and he suddenly seemed completely at ease, and then, so was she. After that, their association took on a closeness—a trusting camaraderie that seemed even an improvement over their already respectful bond.

* * * * *

In the next few weeks Amanda began to absorb as much of the business as she could. She kept checking out a number of books from the library. Books with titles that led her to believe they held the keys to the great mysteries of finance and the handling of money. Mr. C. picked up a book once and asked her if she understood her studies, if they were clear to her. After that, she felt free to ask him some questions about things that were a problem to her. She did most of her studying after supper when Mr. C. had retired for the night, but she never asked him anything until the next day. She never knocked on his door for any reason. She marked passages that were not clear to her some of the time and brought them up the next day, usually at their lunch break. They ate at the store at noon most of the time, as he seemed reluctant to leave her to eat alone at the store while he went home. She asked one time if he felt their lunches were as healthy for him as Mrs. Barrett's cooking, and he said, "You may not find them so, but as long as we eat some fruit and raw vegetables along with my peanut-butter-and-banana sandwiches and your cheese and sardines, we'll survive." Caught off guard again at his wit, she laughed until she hurt. Her cheese and sardines, yeah?

She never mentioned the loss of school, nor did she ask if she could have continued there. She felt it was better she was learning the business. She felt satisfied she was busy with things she would need to know, if and when she was left with the whole thing. The business she would run when Mr. C. was gone, or had become incapacitated—too sick to make decisions.

Miss Quaid, her English and Government teacher when she had been in school, seemed very pleased she was doing some studies and said, "Amanda, you must keep on with some education. You have a wonderful mind, and your grammar is excellent; it's much better than most of the students we've had all along. Some day you will want to continue your education, and remember, you don't have to have a high school diploma to get into a college. They have a sub-college certificate. Once you pass the test, you can feel free to take all the college courses you want. Some wonderful teachers are out there now, teaching on a subcollege certificate and working toward degrees each summer."

With that said, Miss Quaid, the middle-aged spinster teacher that some folks thought was haughty, picked up her sack of groceries and went out the door. Amanda was so stunned she walked around in a daze the rest of the day. Mr. C. never mentioned hearing of Miss Quaid's remarks, but Amanda believed he had. His temperament those days was even and, at times, jovial, and his steps, she felt, were lighter than they had been when she had first known him.

Anyway, she became more determined to learn all she could without letting her work at the store slide. She could not, *would not*, do that. She made a solemn vow to herself and the Lord to take as much work as possible, and everything else she could, from her lovely Mr. C.'s shoulders. She felt he needed to be here at work every day, as he seemed to enjoy his time at his business with his people, but she insisted on his rest periods. She kept an eagle eye on him to see he did not lift heavy sacks or stay in any conversation with any customer if it was the least bit upsetting. Those unpleasant conversations only happened once in a great while, as most of their customers were Mr. C.'s friends. They knew Mr. C. was honest in all his dealings and as fair as a man could possibly be.

Chapter 4

As winter set in, the town plodded along with so little change that Amanda, out of boredom, counted the days until Christmas. She realized Christmas would be very different this year, more than any she had ever been involved in before.

One night at supper, when Bubba brought Christmas into the conversation, Mr. C. said, "Shall we have a tree?"

And Amanda asked, "Oh, could we?"

That became their project from then on. There were decorations, and with Bubba and an axe, there was finally a lopsided tree in the living room. As it turned out, she and Bubba did the decorations. He became so excited and hyperactive that she had to see after each ball and light that went up. She helped him choose each one and decide exactly where each of them went. It took several evenings after supper, and once or twice, Mrs. Barrett went across to her house and left Bubba and Amanda involved with the tree. This was a change in Mrs. Barrett's habits; before she had Bubba go along home when Mr. C. retired for the night. Amanda felt almost giddy when she realized Mrs. Barrett was getting more trusting with her, especially where her association with Bubba was concerned.

When she had joined Mr. C. for meals, the Barretts had eaten in the kitchen, and Amanda had wondered why Bubba had been so puzzled about the arrangement. Then, when she brought up the subject, Mr. C. had asked if she minded if the Barretts took their meals with them, and she felt free to say "yes." Since they now ate together and had family conversations, Amanda felt a lot less strain between herself and Mrs. Barrett and was happier with the meal.

Since they were having a tree, Amanda realized they should have presents. What good was a tree if there were no wrapped gifts to put under it? She wondered how she could manage to get gifts for the three others in the household, to let them know she cared about them. She could not sew, and that was what her mother had done. She had made clothes for her and her dad. Her present had usually been a new blouse, skirt, dress, or jacket her mother had made, and there usually had been a new western-type shirt or jacket for her dad.

She had no idea what a suitable gift for Mr. C. would be; he had clothes enough to change many times for work, for church, and for town meetings. Every once in a while, he still came out on Sunday morning in something she had not seen before.

As time for the holiday drew nearer, she became terribly downcast at her inability to find something she could give this wonderful man, and that was all she could think of now. She wished one of them could have a wrapped present for Bubba, as he was actually a child, with all the wonder and awe children found in the spirit of Christmas. The same awe had been in his eyes when he had seen a lovely flower, a colorful rainbow, or a beautiful sunset.

Then one night, after supper, Mr. C. looked at her and asked if she would like to take an afternoon off and go to Greenville, shopping. She looked at him and said, "Can we afford to do that?"

He said, "I know you can, as you have not paid yourself any wages since we married."

The Amanda said, "You said we are partners, and partners don't pay themselves wages."

"Oh, but they do. Or at least, I pay myself, so why not you?" He smiled that wonderful smile again.

"I didn't know you pay yourself. There's no record on the books…" She looked away and stopped her words, if not her thoughts.

"Right. I just slip some money out occasionally when I need it for the little lockbox."

"But you don't spend any money much. Just when we eat out, and that's for me as much as for you," she said.

"I had so many clothes when the Depression happened I've not needed anything to wear, and if my clothes are out of date, so are most people's. Right?"

On Friday afternoon they left the store with Thomas and drove over to the biggest town in the area, which was Greenville. Amanda had not known there was any place outside of the fabled Dallas with so many stores and so many different kinds of stores. She had expected a larger town than Canesville, but all the things in the show windows were mind-boggling. A lot of them she had never seen except in the Sears and Roebuck catalogue. She was astounded at the many different things, and then there was a great big sign across the Main Street that proclaimed "Greenville—The blackest land and the whitest people. Welcome to Greenville."

She needed to have some idea of what Mr. C. would like to have, so she carefully watched as he window-shopped along the sidewalks. She felt so ignorant because she knew nothing about a man's preference in gifts. Her daddy had always only been interested in western-type things; his eyes always lit up when he looked at anything western, even spurs. His interest ran to bolo ties, western shirts, riding pants, and belts with western-type buckles. She had never seen Mr. C. wear anything western and did not think he wanted anything in that line.

Finally, she asked if he would help her shop for him, and he said he would if she would do the same for him. Their next stop was at a jewelry store, and she was astounded at the beautiful array of lovely watches, necklaces, rings, bracelets, and other bangles. "Maybe," she thought, "he guessed I might like one of the little lockets I have seen other girls wear on bright, shiny chains." She had never mentioned the locket to her parents, as she had felt there never would be enough money to buy one for her, and her dad would have thought the whole idea of a bauble for her was silly. She had hidden her wish for one away in her daydreams after she had seen other little girls wearing them.

When they were in the store, a man came forward and shook Mr. C.'s hand and asked how he was. Also, he stood quietly while Mr. C. introduced him to Amanda as his wife. He had called Mr. C. Herbert. Herbert? And had shaken her hand too. Mr. C. told her he and this man had gone to Normal School together, that they were personal friends. Amanda had not known Mr. C. had gone to college and said so, but the man explained Normal School was not really college at that time, even though it was a seat of some higher learning.

When she turned to stand by Mr. C. at the counter, she was surprised when he pointed and the jeweler took out a tray of gold wedding bands. She had tried to see if, by chance, Mr. C. was interested in a ring, but was shocked the tray was filled with all ladies' rings. She backed away and hid her hands behind her.

Mr. C. said, "I am sorry you have had to wait so long for your ring. I'm sorry I've not taken the time to take care of this before now. Would you let Bryce measure your finger?" She still could not bring her work-scarred hands out for both men to see. Her face was beet red, and she could not speak. The question on her face and her inability to speak must have warned Mr. C., because he asked the man to wait. Taking her by the shoulders, he gently led her to the far corner of the store and said, "Amanda, you are my wife, and you should have had a ring when we were first married. Last week I got jolted out of my neglect when two nosy ladies looked for a ring on your finger. Finding none, they just looked at each other and shrugged. Do you see now?" And of course, she did. She knew from her books the proper thing to do was for them to each get a ring, and that is what they did.

To her, the cost was staggering, but Mr. C. said he did not get one when he married the first time and laughed and said, "At least they are a good investment." The storeowner used no pressure and seemed to enjoy their shopping, but he sided with Amanda when she said she needed a heavy, plain band, a lot like the man's ring that Mr. C. chose. She knew anything fancy would make a mockery of her wide, work-scarred hands. The hands that had taken a lot of abuse and neglect needed nothing tiny and feminine to bring attention to them. They ended up with plain fourteen-carat matching gold bands with no engraving except their initials on the inside.

The fact that the man named Bryce Thompson called Mr. C. Herbert put him in the same age group with her wonderful husband, and she hoped the man knew she loved her husband dearly. He would never be Herbert or Herb, not just because of an unpopular president, but because he had earned respect from everyone who knew him. He would be her wonderful Mr. C. She believed Mr. Thompson did know, because he hugged them both and asked that they come by again—anytime—and to keep him posted about what went on in Canesville.

Before the stores closed, they bought Mrs. Barrett some shoes, house shoes, and flannel for her to use to make sleeping garments for herself and Bubba. They bought Bubba some fleece-lined coveralls, work boots, and a fairly high-powered flashlight. All in all, they felt satisfied with their shopping and went to a fancy (to her) restaurant to eat their evening meal.

Mr. C. insisted she try some food she had not eaten before, so she finally settled on a broiled T-bone steak and a lovely tossed salad. She had always had steak chicken-fried with gravy, so she slowly cut into the bubbling, tender steak and tasted it as Mr. C. watched her closely. He was very pleased when she ate the bite and then attacked the rest of the steak with gusto.

On the way home, Mr. C. hummed and then outright sang one of his favorite hymns. Then he looked at her and said, "Do you know any carols besides 'Jingle Bells?'" And suggested they sing a carol together. They sang together side by side on Sunday mornings, and each knew the voice range of the other, so it was easy to pick a song that was right for their voices.

They sang "It Came Upon the Midnight Clear," and to her, they harmonized just fine. It seemed a miracle they were here, under a plush velvet sky set with a million diamond-like stars, in a softly purring automobile that protectively enclosed them. The whole arc of the sky seemed to enclose them with peace and beauty and all the blessings they had. She felt the blessings were sent to Mr. C., and she only shared them because of this wonderful, loving man. She also felt she could reach up and touch one of the stars, and then it would lead her to Bethlehem. The very brightest, she knew, was still standing over the stall where the Baby Jesus had lain in a manger. The word pictures and imagery in her brain kept materializing about that even as they sang other carols and hymns.

Later, Mr. C. sang some silly songs she had never heard before, some nonsensical ditties, and they both became as silly as two kids. Mr. C. did "Where have you been, Billy Boy?" and Amanda came in on "She's a young thing and cannot leave her mother" at the end of each verse. This indeed was a part of this wonderful man she would never have guessed he had. She knew he was as comfortable to be with as anyone she had ever known, but this peek into the inside workings of his non-workaday mind was an entertaining part of him. He made her laugh with little puns and sayings. Some she would not have recognized as wit had she not seen the quirky lifting of the corners of his lips and the fringes of humor in his eyes. The imagery of "I Never See Maggie Alone" was so hilarious when he came to "They were huggin' and kissin' when the old car got to missin'. He jumped out as quick as he could, raised up the hood, and there was her father, her mother, her sister and her brother! Oh, I never see Maggie alone." She laughed until she was weak.

Now he seemed to enjoy her company. He wanted to see her let go of her tenseness and the feeling of inferiority that had been with her all of her life. At last, he told her about her great ability to learn and reason. He promised her she could walk in any crowd and be assured she was capable of being and doing anything she wanted.

She, in turn, told him he was the finest person she had ever known. She wondered aloud why God had given her into his care: the one person in the entire world she would have chosen to be her husband, brother, and friend. Of all men, everywhere, in all the different ages she had studied, this man would have been her very first choice. She knew she would have chosen him in any and all areas of her existence. He was the hero of all her daydreams.

Then he said, "You forgot 'father,' and that's where I would have fit the best."

When she objected strenuously, he asked if she would like to cruise on up to DC and visit with Franklin and Mrs. Eleanor in front of the fire before they slept in the Lincoln room. She laughed until they were home, and the frost bit her nose as they left the comfort of the car and entered the warm, friendly house. She had still looked at the brightest star and wondered why life had been so good to her at this time when so many others were in dire need. She wished with all her heart she could always have this wonderful man to know and love. She did love him, and she told him so.

He said, "I know you do, Amanda, and I am so pleased and feel so humble. I have prayed you would learn about love, as you have had so little of it in your life. Since you have now opened your heart and have some love there, let it grow. Let it expand, and you will find places for many people and much, much more love. That will bring you joy and happiness."

"But how will I learn when people close their hearts and minds, just as my parents did? Is it safe to open up to those who can and will reject me?" she asked.

"In the beginning you may feel rejection, but if you find one who accepts you and what you have to offer, count that as a victory. You have already proved you can care for the unlovely, and that is the hardest thing in life to do. I have watched you with Bubba, your respect of his feelings and patience of his mistakes. You will always enjoy his love and respect for all time to come, as long as he lives, and there'll be others as you take up my work."

Then he said, "My little work to make life a little easier for some people is my dream. I knew when I started it I could not be a benefactor to many, yet I have felt compelled to share what I could with a few. I have seen the sorrow on fathers' and mothers' faces when they were suffering because they could not find a way to get the much-needed wholesome food and even the medications for their children.

"If you undertake this, I want you to promise me you will do what you can for some and not fret and fume for the many who are needy that you can't find the money to give to. If you fall into that way of thinking, of wanting to do it on a big scale, it will make you sick, thereby taking away your ability to help those that are the most destitute. Can you promise me to do what you can and go easy on yourself?" And of course, she made the promise and felt the vow was as binding as their marriage vows.

Then she asked, "Mr. C. who taught you to be so loving and giving?"

And he said, "I had a very openly Christian father and mother. I was raised in a home that believed love was sharing with others as a testimony for our love of God Himself. It has been easy for me most of the time because it was the very essence of the family life that I grew up sharing with family members." So they entered their warm, friendly home, said "good night," and went to their separate rooms to bed.

*****

The next few days were happy for Amanda, and it seemed it went through the whole household. Mrs. Barrett seemed a little less acidic, and less open with letting Amanda know she felt it was not right for Amanda to be equal to Mr. C. H. Connor. Bubba was fit to be tied. He wanted to open his gifts immediately. She explained Santa Claus had left them there so they would be safe until Christmas morning, and if they were opened now, they might just disappear to the North Pole. Then he decided he would not open them, but could he take them home to sleep with them?

Amanda had not been around children except at church and school. She knew Bubba had been trainable because his mother had taught him. Most of the time, he remembered his table manners and remembered not to track in dirt, without being chided. Mr. C. had taught him to do some work at the store. He kept the yard and did some hoeing and raking to help his mother in the vegetable garden and with the flowers. Being in this household, she wondered why her mother and father had never played word games with her, talked to her about puzzles or riddles, or played games with her.

The new garments her mother had made for her at Christmas had been welcome to stretch her scanty wardrobe, and she had been grateful for them. They had been plain, never fussy or decorated with lace or frills. They had been neatly made, along with some underwear, from some soft, white flour sacks. They had helped her to feel clean and respectable.

Once she found a new three-quarter length coat, made from some heavy sail cloth with cotton sateen lining, at the foot of her bed on Christmas morning. That was the Christmas that she was twelve. She had a growth spurt and knew the three-quarter length was so if she grew fast the next year, the hemline would not be noticeable.

She did remember finding a tiny doll once, on a Christmas morning, in her shoe. It was lying in a bed made of sprigs fashioned into the shape of a cradle. She never mentioned the doll to anyone because she did not know who had put it there. She wondered if her mother had given it to her. If her father found out about it, he would be angry about the cost of it. She kept it in her desk, which she had made from orange crates.

The desk had two orange crates standing on end about fourteen inches apart, with a board across the tops of them nailed in place. The space between the crates was an opening for her knees. She had intended to gather material around the front to hide her papers on the shelves that were the dividers in the crates. She wondered now if the little desk was still in what had been her bedroom, and if the little doll was still in the cradle.

Once, while Amanda was in the store alone, her father came in, and she noticed how gaunt he looked and how very nervous he seemed. He walked to her, and she stood and waited. She was not afraid; she just waited for him to speak. He moved his feet around, cleared his throat, and said, "Amanda, I know you are holding the things I did and said against me, and I can understand that. I wish I could go back and undo those things I did and said, but I can't do that...I wish I could." And he turned and walked away, out the door. She had been too stunned to speak.

She knew he had been in the store before; she had seen his charge tickets, not often, but he had bought groceries. The night after she saw him, before she went to sleep, she looked up and asked God to help her, if not to understand her parents, then to give her the grace to forgive them.

Her mother had gone to town very seldom in her lifetime and since the Depression hardly at all. That meant Amanda had no way to find out if she was all right. She wished she had asked her dad about her mother, if she was well…She wondered if she still wore the navy blue alpaca dress she always wore to church. She thought if she did, maybe she had made a new collar and cuffs for it. The collar and cuffs on it had been taken off and laundered until they were turning yellow with age and so many washings and ironings. She wondered if her mother still went to church on Sundays, and if she still played the piano for the services. She had nothing at home to practice music on, as their piano had been one of the first things sold after the Depression began. Amanda had not ever understood why her mother stayed on in that house, accepting anything her husband did and said. She had not understood it back as far as she could remember, but Amanda had never had the courage to ask any questions. She supposed her mother stayed because she had no place to go nor any job or job skills to make a living for herself and for her child—Amanda. Without a child, maybe her mother could have escaped the neglect and emotional abuse of her father's tongue. The thought almost made her ill.

Most of the time, her mother had left the house only on Sunday mornings and never appeared to resent her husband's erratic comings and goings. She had worked at keeping the little house livable, the meals edible, and all their clothes wearable. She was unapproachable about her marriage, not to just Amanda, but to everyone. Now Amanda wished she could have accepted that about her mother. Amanda would have insisted on a discussion about not just her parents' marriage, but marriage in general. She wish she could have been a child who could have crossed the line of her mother's stolidity and found some warmth, or she could have shown some warmth and understanding. Her mother may not have had either of those characteristics, but Amanda wished she, herself, had tried to see why her mother had not had them. She promised the Lord, and herself, that one day she would go to her mother and ask why she had let life bog her down to the point that she had very little pleasure in life and, it seemed, very little to live for.

Then she wondered if her mother had reading material. That would be one thing she could do for her without getting involved with her parents. She could buy her mother a book or subscribe for her a magazine or two.

When she asked Mr. C. about their finances, he immediately told her they could afford presents for her parents. Then she said, "My mother loves to read, and I thought I might buy her a book or two or subscribe to a ladies' magazine for her."

"That is a wonderful idea. Why don't we do both? I wondered if maybe J. M. might like one of those lined jackets."

"No." She shook her head and said, "He has plenty of clothes, and Mother has almost nothing decent to wear, even to church on Sunday. I won't add to the inequity that has always been between those two."

"So," he said, "we can get her a dress too."

She hesitated for a time, to try to make her answer make sense, and then she said, "I don't want them to think I am trying to buy their good feelings or to show them I'm in better circumstances than they are. The magazines will be enough, and to set the record straight, I am not resentful about things I don't understand. I don't hate or despise either of them. The Lord has been so good bringing me into your life, and I am so thankful for…Really, if I know they have enough to eat and a roof over their heads, then I'm satisfied. They will survive, for they know how to manage for food and the necessities. Maybe I should feel guilty I have so much, but I don't. I am just thankful."

Mr. C. looked her in the eye and said, "I am very proud of you, Amanda. You have shown me again there are things in this world that makes it imperative we care for others as we can, and when we are really needed. We must believe in goodness and mercy, and if you can accept those people who refused to accept you and your problems, then it shows you will eventually forgive them. That will be selflessness and altruism at its best."

The Amanda said, "What does that word mean?"

He laughed and said, "You don't have to worry about it, because it is alive and well in your heart. It is unselfish care and interest in others." She began to see the glitter of humor in his eye as he added, "It is looking Mrs. Barrett in the eye and refusing to hear criticism, but having the patience to wait for explanations she didn't believe you would wait to hear."

And the fringes of humor were in his eyes, and she looked amazed. He said, "You didn't believe I saw what she was trying to get by with."

"Then, if you knew those things were going on, why didn't you say something?" She glared at him.

"The truth of the matter was, you were doing OK with no interference from anyone. Had she ever gotten nasty, I mean hurtful, I would have called her hand. Really, I think you have won, not just the battle, but the war."

Then he smiled, and so did she. For the first time, he pushed his hands up to her shoulders and gave her a squeeze. Instead of looking up to him and saying "Thank you," she turned her face into the solid comfort of his shoulder to hide her tears. She wondered why she had to tear up and cry when he offered her understanding and ease. That ease had a special essence, and she realized she loved this man more than anyone she had ever known.

He had filled her heart where there had been only emptiness. He had taught her the joy one could have if his or her life was used to bring hope to others and to make that the prime object of one's life.

Then she raised her head, and the swimming, deep blue eyes searched his face, and she asked, "Who taught you such wonderful and dedicated service?"

The answer he gave was soft and hesitant. "I was raised in a very truly and openly Christian home. Both my parents were dedicated to God and the welfare of others. In watching your folks and the empty childhood you had, I wanted to make your life a little fuller and watch you climb to a better belief in yourself and others. I had no intentions of bringing you into my personal life and certainly not my home." She tried to interrupt, but he continued, "That happened by accident, or rather by my misunderstanding. I am glad it did happen. It has been a pleasure, and when I leave you, I know you will do your very best to finish what I have begun, if you can."

Then he went on his way without letting her castigate herself for what she considered her misleading him about being in trouble.

Chapter 5

One night, after the Barretts had gone home, Amanda heard Mr. C. close the door to the basement stairs and saw he had a metal box in his hands. He sat beside her on the sofa and unlocked the box with a very small key that was tied to a string. He opened the box and looked at her solemnly. "Oh, no," she thought. "He must think his time is getting short, or he wouldn't bring this up so close to bedtime."

She hated the idea he thought it was necessary for him to explain the workings of the little box and how she was to go about the bank business. How could she, an ignorant little girl, know how to carry on this project?

Then he said, "Amanda, these shares on top are made out to the names on them." He lifted the packet that was tied with a rubber band. Some of them are men who may need money later. If they do, you are, as far as possible, to lend them what is absolutely needed, and let them sign the shares over to you as collateral.

"There is a move afoot for the government to buy people's cows, and some may prefer to sell them to the government. They can't do that if the cows are mortgaged. If they know you intend for them to pay their banknotes and let them keep their cows, it will be better. Because the government is supposed to kill the cattle they buy and bury them. So nobody will get any good out of the deal except the little bit of money the government pays the owners of the cows. I think they are paying about six to ten dollars a head. The bank may sell the ones they confiscate because the people haven't been able to meet their banknotes."

Amanda's breath hissed through her teeth, and she said, "Buy, kill, and bury the cows? Why in the world would they do that when there are hungry people right here as well as in all the world!"

"The group in Washington is trying to figure out how to reduce the number of livestock so they can be worth more on the so-called cattle market. Then the meat producers will begin to make a profit and will get more for the meat and meat products, above the cost of feed and maintenance. Enough to eke out a living."

"Well, they are crazy!" she fumed. "I see every day in the store when people come to buy the staples that they have already been to Battletons' Produce and sold their milk, cream, eggs, chickens, and butter. When their cows are gone, that only leaves the chickens to help them buy the necessities for the making of meals. With the cows going, so will a large part of their income—and the best part of their diet—it will be gone too. Right? I may be ignorant about a lot of things, especially business, but even I can see this is plain stupidity."

Mr. C. looked at her with a real smile on his face and said, "I think you have just proven you are not ignorant, and you care about our folks in our trade area. So let's get on with this." And his smile was open and warm, just as if he had been assured his plans for the future of the community were in the right hands.

"These second packets of shares are those I have redeemed already. The holders have signed them over to me. Judge Halsey drew up the papers and witnessed the exchange of the ownership, and all have the seal of a notary public. That should preclude any objections that they are bogus or there has been any coercion used to get them. If there should be any hearing or suit brought against you in the future about them, just turn it all over to the judge and John. They will know how to handle it. They will be handling my will and guiding you in everything else anyway.

"Now, these shares belong to some families that are a little better off than others; they may not approach you for help. Later, if some are really suffering, I suggest you ask if things are really bad and offer money. If he—they—reject the offer because of pride, I suggest you ask him if it was true I took bank shares as security. If he says he thinks so, then invite him to Halsey's office and let Hap or John explain it. Do you think you can sit and listen as if you are learning something new?" And of course, she said she could, and Mr. C. had his smile back in place.

In fact, she allowed she probably could learn more by listening to the lawyers than what Mr. C. had explained to her so far. Mr. C. told her to listen to each transaction, to try to see and understand who was truly needy and who might have heard about it as a giveaway and wanted something for nothing. "You only learn to read people by keeping an open mind and by weighing their feelings about things that are being discussed."

Then Amanda asked, "Why are you doing this when we know you can handle it much better than I can and be a lot less likely to make mistakes?"

Then Mr. C. said, "Amanda, look me in the eye and listen: You will be handling my business, and I believe you will let Hap Halsey and John guide you. However, you will be making decisions that are very important to this community. Maybe this will be too much for you. If, when you get into it, you think so, the time to say so will be then, because it is making you ill. OK?"

Then she made up her mind. She realized Mr. C. thought she could do it. So she would do her dead level best to see it through. She felt if he had not thought she could handle it, he would have turned it over to his very capable lawyers and friends—one friend who had served on a judge's bench when he had been needed.

She looked this very solemn man in the eye and said, "I will do my very best to do what you want done, *but*, you are not fooling me for one moment. This is your way to continue my education, and I am terrified. I have never failed a test in school yet…though I think I have failed all of the other tests in my life that have come my way."

"Never, Amanda. You haven't failed at anything, and I know you are good, unselfish, and kind. I have watched you in my business and in this home, and I feel you are capable and have a very keen mind and a will to grow in knowledge and wisdom."

He arose from the sofa, took the little metal box, and went down the basement stairs. She sat in a ball in her chair and did not follow him to see where he put the box.

For some reason, she had an unsettled feeling and wondered why Mr. C. had felt compelled to explain the box and bring out his plans for the times he would not be here. During their months of sharing his home and business, she had never heard him complain. The only times she had felt a real concern for his health were when he lost color and appeared tired. When that happened, she became very adamant he was to stop what he was doing and lie down to rest. Tonight, he had not appeared to be tired and worn out, but rather his color was flushed instead of ashen.

When he was leaving to go to his bedroom he paused at the living room door and said, "Good night, Amanda."

And she looked in his dear face and said, "Good night, Mr. C."

At about midnight, she came wide-awake and knew she had heard a noise. She jumped from the bed and flew to the door of his bedroom. When she got to his door and pushed on the light, she saw he was twisted and in terrible pain. She ran down, picked up the phone, rang Beatrice Clemons at Central, and told her to call Dr. Story and Ben Miles, the sheriff. Then, her mind in turmoil, she flew to unlock the back door. She went to his bed, sat by him, and held his head and shoulders in her arms and begged him not to leave her. He seemed to know she was there and was trying to say something. She believed, with all her heart, it was the word "love." She said, "I love you so much, and I need you so much. Please don't leave me now; I am not ready. I need you so much, and I love you more than I can tell you!"

Then he tried again to say something, but the corner of his mouth had fallen down. She put her ear to his lips, and the best she could believe he was saying was "box" and something else she could not make out in the garbled sound.

His eyes began to roll, and in a frenzy, she cried to him, "Stay with me, Mr. C. Don't leave me now. I need you." And her tears fell onto his head, and she rubbed them from his face and from hers as she cried out her loss to the only person who had really loved her. He did say another word, but her mind did not record it.

Then she knew he was not breathing, and she turned his head and tried to get him to take another breath. She had never seen death come to a person before, but she recognized it and loathed it. She could not watch it now, so she laid her head on his and said, "Why, God? Why? Why couldn't he stay? Why couldn't he stay until I am old enough and have learned enough to do what needs to be done? He has been my salvation, and I am grateful, but…why not take some worthless person instead of the finest man I have known?" And her tears were running down her cheeks and her dear Mr. C.'s face.

And then Dr. Story was holding her and letting her cry against his chest. When she realized who he was, she pulled away and yelled at him to do something for her Mr. C., to bring life back to him.

And then Dr. Story said, "There is nothing I can do. I am sorry. He knew and accepted this, and yet he did all he could. I did all I could do to postpone it. He did stay longer than we thought possible, because he knew you needed him. He stayed because he thought of all the good you could do if he could be here to teach you. You do realize that, don't you?" He drew back and gazed into her swimming, dark eyes, and she did realize that. Her wonderful husband had given her enough teaching and training to do some of the things he had dreamed of her doing. So she moved aside and let the undertaker and Ben Miles load her loved one onto a litter and carry him out of the house for the last time. She realized she was back where she had been before her life in this house had started. When her parents had rejected her, and the town kids had hunted her, just as they would hunt an animal. He had truly protected her and had kept her safe, and now he would not be here to be her guide and protector anymore.

What in the world would she do now? He had told her the house was hers, and she knew, if she could keep it, she would always love it and take care of it. He did say half the store was hers; they ran it as a fifty-fifty endeavor.

She had no idea who would be her partner now. He had told her that the money for the banking business he was carrying on came from the store, so evidently, he had meant she should use funds from the business to keep the bank shares moving into her hands.

She went to her bedroom, caught a glimpse of herself in the mirror on her dresser, and realized she had on nothing but her gown. It was flannel and was thick enough to cover her fairly well. Besides, she had done what she had to do, and that had been to go with Mr. C. as far as she could when he was leaving her. She knew she was going to be lonely and felt emptiness and a very unsettled ripple of fear.

She thought maybe she should dress before sunrise, as some people might be coming to pay their respects. As had she and Mr. C. when Mr. Castleton had died some months ago. She had gone with him to pay their respects (he had said) to the home and again to the funeral service. She had not looked at Mr. Castleton after he was dead, so she knew this was a completely new experience for her. Amanda wondered if anyone would pay respects to the one who now was gone. She knew many people in the town and county had liked and respected him, so the only question was, did they respect her enough to pay tribute and honor to Mr. C. and his home with her here? She did not know what the people thought of her. She had tried to be respectable and had worked hard to be a credit to a wonderful man who had cared a lot about her, as anyone could see by his actions.

When Mrs. Barrett and Bubba came to the house, Amanda told them how it had happened and asked what she should do. What would be expected of her, and would Mrs. Barrett not just take over the running of the household but also guide her in what she was to do? What did Mrs. Barrett think needed to be done? The lady who at first had resented her had a face on her that strongly suggested sympathy for Amanda and hurt and loss for herself and Bubba. Bubba wept and asked, "Mr. C. left? Mr. C. gone to heaven?" And the last was a heartrending question. Both Amanda and his mother put their arms around him and assured him, in every way they could, that Mr. C. had indeed gone to heaven.

Then the people came, bringing food, cards, and handpicked flowers made into arrangements, and then, later in the jumbled up day, the undertaker called and said the body was ready for viewing. She felt paralyzed; she did not feel able to go to see him again all twisted in pain and pasty white. Mrs. Barrett saw what the problem was and asked if they could all go. She had been home and had put on her second-best dress, and Bubba had combed his hair and changed his shirt. Amanda then took a moment to talk to herself, and she finally felt ready to go and do what she had to do. She knew Mrs. Barrett and Bubba were the ones closest to him, except for herself. She told them so and suggested they be Mr. C.'s and her next of kin.

When they arrived at the store, Mr. Clem Saunders met them at the front door and escorted them to the viewing room. It was at the back of the hardware and furniture store. She approached the casket with dread, but when Mr. Saunders backed away to let them have privacy to go up to see him, Amanda was amazed at the difference in him. He looked well; there was color in his cheeks, and it seemed there was a hint of a smile around his mouth. She felt this was Mr. C. and had no fear or dread. She smiled right back at him. She stepped up closer and ran a hand on his hands. He was cold to touch, but she very softly patted his cheeks and told him silently how much she loved him, and she hoped he heard and understood her.

When she turned to Mr. Saunders, she asked, "How did you manage to bring him back to his sweet and pleasant self?"

And the man said, "That is one of the things that keeps my job from being unbearable."

"When do I take care of the bills and set a funeral hour?" she asked.

Mr. Saunders said, "That has all been taken care of. You see, C. H. had known for a while this was coming—not someday, but soon. You can change anything you want, but he had asked, in his plan, that only one full day was to pass before his services, so that would call for tomorrow. Maybe at two?" he suggested. Then he said, "And the suit you picked out and sent up here looks just right, don't you think?"

Then she nodded and said, "You have done a wonderful job. Er...I had thought he would look like he did last night—so..." She twisted her hands. "When am I to take care of the bills?"

"Everything is taken care of. When Mrs. Leona died, he decided to make his own arrangements, as they had no children. She had no family, and he had only one brother he wasn't close to."

"What is his brother's name, and where is he? Where can I locate him?" And she was mystified when Mr. Saunders seemed hesitant to answer.

Then he looked her in the eye and said, "I will try to contact him if you insist, but C. H. had told me to put him under with only his wonderful friends, neighbors, and church family to bid him goodbye."

"Then that is what we will do. Do you mean to tell me he paid for his care and his funeral services?"

"Yes, that's right, and he came to see me again after you were married, and we discussed the way he had everything set up. His real concern was that he didn't want you to have any trouble at all with anything. But if you really wanted to change anything, I was to do it."

"Wasn't he a wonderful person?" And she went back to the casket to look him in the face and tell him again how much she loved him.

To be a young teenager when her life had changed so drastically, most of the folks in the town thought Amanda managed fairly well. A lot of them showed up at the house and were greeted by Amanda, Mrs. Barrett, or Bubba. There was always coffee in the pot or iced tea in the refrigerator and some kind of cake, cookies, and pies that many people brought to the house. Bubba was always there to try to help and was heard to say often that Mr. C. was a wonderful guy.

Amanda had wondered many times that long, awful day if Bubba had heard her say, when she was talking to the undertaker, that same thing—if not, she knew in her heart it was true. Mr. C. was indeed a wonderful man.

The services went along as planned, and Amanda was not surprised at the songs he had chosen, the pallbearers he had named, or the scriptures he asked to be read on the last day—his final service. She knew they were his favorites. It was true she had not known him long, just since the day last summer when he had asked if she was interested in working part-time for him. He had offered part-time in the summer and after school in the fall and winter. She knew deep down in her heart she was different, altogether different, for having known him. She was much better, for he had shown her a new life and a whole new look at life.

So she and her two people, Mrs. Barrett and Bubba, sat together and listened to the minister of Mr. C.'s church explain to all, here had been an exceptional man who lived his religion every day. And she and her adoptive family said, "Amen." She felt the presence of her father and mother at the back of the church, but by the time she went out the back door, they were gone.

The praises for her kind and gentle Mr. C. were appreciated because they were not syrupy and overdone, and Amanda felt that most of the minister's listeners felt that this was a wonderful, clean-living, *gentle man* in the truest sense of the word *gentleman*.

Later, she managed to stay in the living room as long as anybody wanted to visit there, and Mrs. Barrett was gracious about the kitchen and food folks had brought in.

When the last ones were gone, Amanda was exhausted and could see Mrs. Barrett was feeling the long hours of the day. So Amanda suggested Mrs. Barrett and Bubba should go home and let the always-spotless kitchen wait for morning to be scrubbed down. Mrs. Garrett gave in, but she told Amanda only the cups from the last group of coffee drinkers were left in the sink.

Amanda could see Bubba was so tired his face was white, and his eyes were trying to stay open, but he was totally past going on by now. She thanked them both for going through this terrible crisis with her. Something new happened then that had never happened before. Bubba put his arm almost around Amanda and choked up when he tried to say, "Good night."

Then Amanda locked up, went to her room, and just let her mind wander over the events of the last two days. She remembered she had seen her mother and father there, and they had passed by her and hugged her as they followed along for the last viewing. She had no idea how she felt toward them. She was glad they had cared enough to come to pay their respects to Mr. C., and she felt that they felt a sorrow because she had lost the man who had seen enough good in her that he wanted to make her life better.

*****

Amanda sent word to Thomas McGraed to work for her if he could, and he told her he would work full-time until it was time to start a crop. He preferred hourly wages and was always there when trucks were being unloaded and was prompt at loading out customers' wagons or trucks. He kept a record of his hours and had them posted above the cash register. His hourly wages seemed low to her, but it was what Mr. C. had paid him, and he seemed happy with it.

About a week after the funeral, Homes Carter called the store. When she answered, he said, "Amanda, we are having a meeting soon of the bank board, and we need you to bring C. H.'s shares and other bank papers over so we can see where we are at this time. As you know, he was a very good businessman, and we are going to miss him, but we have to pick up and go forward from here."

"I see. When is the meeting and where?"

"The meeting is tomorrow, or as soon as we can have everybody here, but you don't have to worry about that. We just need to look over his shares, get a grip on where we are and how the bank is doing. Do you think you could bring them over this afternoon?"

She said, "I doubt it. I haven't gone through all the papers yet, and it will take a while to find things, sort them, and figure out what everything is. The will is not probated yet, and there are some things I don't understand."

"Well, little girl, that is what we are trying to do, to make it easy for you." And to her that sounded patronizing in his very unctuous voice.

"Who are the 'we,' Mr. Carter?"

"Well, the board. We think we knew C. H. pretty well, and how he would want things to go, to make it easy for you. After all, you are just a young girl and should not have to bother your brain with piddling stuff like this. It's my job, what I am hired to do. Right?"

"Let me think about things and look through some other papers and get my feet on the ground."

"Amanda, how would it be if I come over and help you with some of this? There are two or three different looking papers belonging to the bank, and of course, I am used to seeing all of them. I will recognize them right away." This gracious, good-old-boy attitude was beginning to wear on her nerves, and she did not have much patience left.

The blood started to pound in her head, and she felt pressure behind her eyes, so much she could see waves in front of her face. She felt she might start screaming and never stop. Everything was too much. How could she see to everything? How could she make sense of everything when she could barely do the things that had to be done?

She stopped and started to tell the awful man on the line just what she thought of his suggestions. She stopped, for a picture of J. M. Mason came in front of her eyes, and became almost catatonic.

She waited until her brain got back into gear; she counted to ten. Then she pushed the receiver aside for a second and said, "Oh Lord, I'm sorry!"

She knew to lose it now and blow off steam was not the way to handle this—not as her father would—this was what Mr. C. had trusted her to take care of. Right then she became determined to find his way, the right way, and she would do it.

So she said, "I have a customer; why don't I get back with you tomorrow. Maybe? And thank you for calling." And she hung up the phone. Then she started saying "Snake, crook, hypocrite, villain." None of those words were bad enough, and she would not stoop to that four-word phrase a lot of folks used to describe the lowest life form. She thought even that word would not be evil enough. She went to the restroom, washed her face with cold water, and sat until she could handle the shakes. Right then it seemed Mr. C. was looking down. She grinned a sickly grin because she could almost hear him saying, "See there, I knew that you could do it."

In some way, she felt she might understand her father and his temper fits more than she had before, but she would never accept *his* kind of frustration in *herself*.

When she got home that night, she started thinking she had better go down into the basement and try to find the little metal box. Maybe then she could figure a way to work things out and begin doing what Mr. C. had asked her to do.

She had to have some idea of whether or not the bank had any right to see the papers, and who would make the call about that. Something told her to move very cautiously and s-l-o-w-l-y.

So, first of all, she called Mr. C.'s lawyers to make an appointment to see them. She wanted to talk very little on the telephone, as the operator was always on the line while people were speaking. This called for a short question and a short answer. The judge was apologetic again about her loss and told her he had started work on the probate of will, but there was more to do. She assured him there was no hurry; she needed his help on some other questions. And *soon*. He knew by the stress on that word something had cropped up. He told her to come on over to his office when Thomas came to work the next morning. Once again, she realized there were people who knew and cared about her and what she needed to do.

When she got to the store the next morning and walked into the building from the front door, she immediately felt something was not right. Everything seemed to be in its normal place, but still, it all felt different. She opened the cash drawer, and the odd amount of change was still there. She still had a funny feeling, as if someone had been here and had moved some things around. She pulled out the drawers below the cash register one by one. Nothing she saw looked as if there were things missing, but they were rearranged. She still felt something was different, and the hairs on her neck and her upper arms were standing at attention. For some reason she felt unsettled that someone had invaded her place, her space.

Holding the drawers out one at the time, she saw the charge tickets were still posted on the wire atop a block of wood. The old safe with its rusty, round door ajar still had papers lying inside *almost* in the order she remembered them. She felt the same feeling as she did the night out with Boyd's bunch, hunted and unsafe—terrified. Was her care and protection over, then? The thought made her hands tremble and her knees knock.

Was there no place for her ever again? Was she unguarded and at risk even behind these locked doors?

She was weak, trembling, and almost paralyzed for a bit. Then Thomas came in the door with a bright "good morning." She mastered her thoughts and nerves to ask if it was all right for her to leave all the set-up chores so she could go to the lawyers' office. For some reason she did not mention the feeling she had when she came to work. She really had no evidence, and she did not want to be considered a hysterical girl, paranoid enough to believe everybody was out to do her wrong.

"Of course," Thomas said, "it's no trouble to me. I like to stay busy." So she picked up her purse and walked down the street to the Halseys' office.

When she got into the waiting room, she sat and hoped it would be a bit before they called her to go into the office proper; she wanted her nerves to settle, needed to get control and quit shaking.

Then John Halsey, the son of the judge, said, "Come in, Mrs. Connor." Then he said, "Must I call you Mrs. Connor?"

And she said, "Of course not."

Then he looked at her and said, "Is there something wrong, Amanda, or are you this white in the face and shaken up all the time now?" She gave up on her vow to be businesslike, and her stoicism fled.

"Mr. Halsey." He shook his head and said, "John. I am John."

"John, there are some things happening Mr. C. tried to prepare me for. I think you and your father are to be my counselors, but will you be my friends?" That sounded a solemn and serious question, and she meant it to be. She had to know, and the only way to find out was to ask. She was pretty sure of the Halseys, as she knew Mr. C. trusted them, both father and son, to handle his business. From what he had told her, they had been in on the use of people's bank shares as collateral for loans. They were the only ones who knew the extent of his philanthropy, his trades to assure some of the hungry of this area would be fed, a way for them to get help without feeling they had sold their souls for a mess of pottage.

John nodded his head and said, "We will not only be your friend, but we will see that the things C. H. feared would happen to you, won't."

She told John about the telephone calls from Holmes Carter, and his face turned a fiery red—almost as red as his hair.

"No wonder you are pale this morning."

"That's not all. You probably will think I am paranoid, but someone was in the store last night. I have no evidence, no proof whatsoever. Nothing was taken that I could tell. The change left in the register was there, but somebody had opened the drawers under the cash register where a lot of papers, utility bills, tax receipts, etc. are kept."

"But the bank shares were not there. Right?" he asked, and she shook her head. "Let me think a minute. Did you say Carter offered to come over and go through the papers?" She nodded. "That he would recognize the shares much easier than you?" She nodded again. "Do you know where the papers are?"

Again she nodded and said, "Mr. C. brought up a little metal box from the basement the night he died. He showed me three packets divided with rubber bands—ones he had already redeemed, and some I needed to offer help to immediately. And then there was a smaller pack that I was to offer help if their circumstances worsened. Those were the proud ones, and I was to be very sure they would not believe the help was charity. He wanted me to understand what he was doing, and I would continue on with his project. He was trying to see that people with little children or sickness in the family could have a way to keep their livestock, because produce from their cattle and chickens was sold for as much money as possible to buy staples. And without their tools and teams, he said, they were sunk.

"Also families, especially the ones with children, needed meals with milk and butter to go with their chickens and eggs to keep them healthy. You two here, in the office, knew what he was trying to do, because he said you drew up the papers. That they were legal and foolproof." She stopped and looked for confirmation.

"Yes, we knew, and we thought it was a wonderful work. Are you sure you want to continue on with it?"

"Yes, definitely. I won't know when and how to do it, because I won't know who is needy and when to offer aid. Mr. C. knew them all, and he found some good and made me see the good in almost everybody, regardless of their shortcomings. I am afraid..." She turned her very caring and eager face to John Halsey, and he almost lost his breath. He had not known until that minute she was beautiful.

Then he said, "Amanda, the first thing we have to do is find that wonderful little box and put it in a safe place. If Carter, or they, were willing to go into your store, they might be just as willing to go into your house."

"Oh, Lord in heaven, please *no!*" And in spite of all she could do, her navy blue eyes with darker rings filled with tears.

"Amanda, look at me. I want you afraid. It is common sense, not a weakness. We want you to take no chances coming to or going home from work. You know Ben Miles? Sheriff Miles? He will be patrolling around your store and your home. I am giving you my home number, Dad's number, and Sheriff Miles's number. If this has to do with Carter, he won't do anything openly or in the light of day. He might go into your house or have someone else go in if he knew you were away, and if the Barretts are gone somewhere. He might have somebody do his dirty work, but I don't know who it is."

"I hope it isn't Boyd Chalmers, because he has sworn to make me pay for getting away from his bunch when we were supposed to be at a class picnic." Amanda shivered and turned almost sick enough to throw up. "What I really want to know is how somebody got into the store. The two-by-four was still across the two back doors; nothing without some real horsepower could have pulled that open, and the front door was locked when I opened it with my key. It's scary, you know."

"How many keys are there to the doors? How many do you have, and how many were in C. H.'s pocket when he died?"

"You know, I don't really know. I had a key to the back door the night I had a date with Howard Huff to go to, supposedly, a class social. I got away from the loud, drinking bunch. If that key had not worked that night, if the two-by-four had been in place, I would have been in the worst kind of trouble imaginable."

"So that was what happened that changed your life so drastically." His face was pulled into a frown, but she sensed his care and concern. "Now the thing we need to do first is get the box and get it to a place of safety."

"Where are we going to keep it? We know Mr. C. felt the vault at the bank was a 'no-way.' He also knew it should not be at the store. That leaves it to you to find a place. Will you do that?" She turned her dark blue eyes to him, with the deeper blue rings around the pupils, so dark they were almost black, and John sat there so entranced he forgot what she had asked him.

"We do have a safe here. It's not the strongest in the world, but no one has a key to this office, because we changed the locks last summer and the keys are accounted for."

"Then you do believe somebody has a key to the store?" She shivered again.

"There is nothing else to believe. I will send Malcolm Martin over to change the locks. Uh, how about during the meeting of the bank board?" And he grinned. Then she smiled right back and told him that might be a perfect time. He said, "I'll walk over to your place after dark tonight."

She said, "The Barretts go home at, or a little before, six." Then she thought that at last, maybe there were people who cared about what she had to do, and that she could depend on them to guide her through these troublesome times. So she thanked John Halsey and the Lord, and went back to work.

The long hours of the afternoon passed, and even though she had a better feeling about her problems with the bank and the security here in the store, she still felt an unease that never really left her. The nicest part of her visit to the lawyers' office was the realization that John Halsey wanted her to be careful from now on, but to trust him and the sheriff to keep her safe. She had never had a friend until Mr. C., yet she felt impelled to believe the Halseys and Ben Miles would do their best to keep her safe from the obnoxious banker and Boyd Chalmers.

When Amanda got home that night, she could tell something was wrong with the Barretts. Mary Barrett's mouth was very tight, and she seemed in a quandary and upset about something. Bubba was hyper in a way that happened only when something had really upset him. Neither ate a lot of supper and seemed in a hurry to leave as soon as possible.

Amanda knew that whatever had happened, she needed to hear it. So she asked quietly, "What has happened? It must be bad, and how can I handle it if I don't know what it is?"

Mrs. Barrett looked at her and said, "A boy stopped Bubba from raking leaves at the back of the garden patch and offered him money to sneak back here after dark to open the basement door and leave it unlocked. It was a lot of money. Big bills, Bubba said, with a lot of zeroes. When he refused to take the money and finally threw them down, the boy got mad and promised to beat him within an inch of his life if he didn't do it, and if he told anybody." Amanda could see the terror in their faces, and she knew it was time to be honest with them. It was also time to ask for help and protection for them all.

"Listen to me carefully, and I will tell you what we have to do. First of all, nobody is mad at you, and nobody is going to hurt or harm either one of you. I think I know who that boy is, and he is sorry and mean. He doesn't have anything against Bubba, and he is a coward. Stay out of his way. Go home before dark and lock your doors. If you believe he is in your neighborhood, call Ben Miles. I am going to talk to the sheriff before bedtime tonight. He will be patrolling your house and mine to see nobody harms us. He, the boy who threatened you, is mad at me, and I think he is working for a man Mr. C. didn't agree with on some city things and other questions. What we have to do now is be very careful and not take chances. OK?"

Mrs. Barrett seemed to question the advice but accepted it, as there was little else that seemed a better choice.

Bubba was so relieved that his facial expression cleared up immediately. He told Amanda he knew Sheriff Miles was his friend and knew where he and his mother lived. The sheriff had chased some boys off from their house once because they were scaring him. Those boys had been silly mean…not like that boy today. He had been really bad mean.

"Maybe you could call Sheriff Miles now? Maybe?" And his eyes were so hopeful and trusting that Amanda asked the Lord to please watch over this boy—who would always be a child—and all of them. How could she have been so self-centered that she had only been concerned about her own questions and problems? Surely she understood her hopes and Mr. C.'s dreams touched many others, and she had to start going toward his goals. If she was to succeed in any way, then she must watch her step and make prayerful decisions.

When the Barretts were gone, Amanda waited for John to arrive. He had said he would come soon after dark. When the knock on the back door sounded, she had a tough time for a minute as her overstressed nerves had her paralyzed, and she had to will her feet to move toward the door. She still peeked out the window enough to see it was John. When she let him in, she said, "I'm sorry to be a 'scaredy-cat,' but I'm really on edge."

And John said, "We want you that way. Don't you remember? I told you we want you afraid so you won't take chances. Has something else happened?"

She told him about the threat to Bubba because he would not open the outside basement door tonight.

"How did you get the whole story from Bubba? He seems to go off in all directions when we ask him about anything."

"Well, it does seem that way, but he had already told his mother about it when I got home. He worshipped and adored Mr. C., and just as soon as he found out I belonged to him, his worship of Mr. C. fell to me. He wants me to play with him at times, and he acts as though we are kids, but if he thinks I need something, he is like a bulldog with a bone. Sometimes he is furious he is handicapped and frets that he can't make things happen and turn out as he wants them to."

"Well, I can see you have a great influence on him; he has needed that for a long time. His mother did a good job raising him to be courteous and to behave like a grown person, and C. H. taught him to do some work and to be responsible about his actions. There have been things, only little bits of time, when he caused any problem, and that was brought on by the actions of the so-called 'normal kids.'"

"I know. He told me about Sheriff Miles running those kids off that were aggravating him. He had that pegged. He said that those boys were silly mean, but this boy today was really awful mean. He is smart that way, because the boy today has no conscience—no idea of right and wrong. I heard him being accused of setting up a gang rape of a poor little girl, and he whooped and laughed about it. He did not deny anything and was trying to set me up for the same thing."

"Oh God, Amanda, is that what started all your problems with your folks? Is that what brought C. H. into your life? I know you had worked for him some, but just out of a clear blue sky, he drove up to Oklahoma and married you with no apologies or explanations to anyone."

"John, let me tell you what happened. This is the first time any-one has heard the whole story. Dr. Story knows some of it, and so does your dad.

"It started when I had a date with Howard Huff to go to a class social down at Pleasant Bluff. Boyd Chalmers was driving his car. His date, Melba somebody, her sister and the sister's date, Johnny Jones, and Howard picked me up for the first date I had ever had. We briefly went by the Bluff to check on the stew, and then Boyd said, 'We'll see you SOBs later,' and he didn't use initials, and Coach Marr had to have heard his gutter language. About that time I knew I was in the wrong crowd."

She told John the whole story and knew just the telling brought her some welcome relief. John listened without comment until she had finished the sorry tale…except she just said, briefly, that due to her father's actions, she did not dare go to the house that was the only home she had ever known.

Then John asked, "If you had it to do over, would you change things?"

"I would wish I had not been so dumb—so stupid to mislead Mr. C. and cause him to take the drastic steps he did. But as far as changing anything after that, I would not want to do anything different. He was a wonderful man, and I loved him dearly. I think I always will. He taught me so much, so very, very much, and the only regret I have is a mix-up in an understanding between the two of us and…that it ended too soon…My time with him ended way too soon."

"What was your error that was so terrible it made C. H. do un-called-for and drastic things?" he asked. "Can you tell me?"

"Well, the second night I spent back in the store, because I had no other place to stay, Mr. C. looked at me and said, 'One question, Amanda, are you in trouble?' And being young and stupid, I said, 'The very worst kind.' And I really thought it was. I had Boyd threatening to abuse me in the very worst way imaginable, my father furious enough to kill me, no home, and no mother to take my part, since she had said only four words when I left her: 'You are ruined forever.'"But none of that was what Mr. C. meant, and I had no inkling of his meaning until he sent me to Dr. Story. I had to go because he insisted. The doctor was as mortified when he tried to examine me, as I was.

"It still took a while, and Mr. C. had to ask that question again for me to see he had expected me to know what he meant. Then I realized he thought I was pregnant. Just how dumb could I be?"

"Amanda, you are not dumb at all. C. H. was from a different generation than yours. That was what he thought you meant when you said you were in trouble. That question will always seem archaic to the younger generations from now on. Dad and I thought he believed you were pregnant when he rushed over here to rewrite his will. We understood he wanted you to have his home and his business, but he asked for a clause that provided for any offspring of yours to be recognized, cared for, and given his name."

"I know. But he was so delighted when he realized I was not in that kind of trouble and admitted he had thought, after knowing me, that if I was pregnant, it had happened against my will. He thought it came from rape, and he loathed the idea. He believed in me that much." And Amanda smiled through her tears.

"Amanda, you made C. H.'s life more pleasant than it had been since he lost Mrs. Leona. He got a boost in his everyday life and made some plans that his life's work would continue. That was the promise you would still try to see, that some of the good people of this area would be helped in a very Christian way. Now the time has come to find the metal box. Right?" And Amanda was so grateful she had this tall, stalwart man to brave the dark, chilly basement with her—to help her in case bad men came to find her down there. She still wondered if someone had a key to her house. The only thing that helped her with that question was, since Boyd had asked Bubba to leave a door open, she doubted they had the key. She wondered if she would ever feel safe again.

It appeared Holmes Carter could do anything in this town that he wanted to do. It seemed that way, as Mr. C. had not openly brought to light that Carter was going for repossessions by the bank with no mercy.

She was glad the new locks were on the store. She might have to stay there at night if something caused her to walk and/or drive the seven blocks home after dark.

In the nearly empty, cavernous basement, John asked her to tell him, as closely as she could, the exact words she thought Mr. C. had said when he was dying. She said, "The one word I am sure of was 'box.'" Then she pondered until one garbled word broke loose from the others in her whirling brain, and she whispered, "'Steps?' Does that make any sense?"

And John studied her and then said, "I think his hiding place may be under this stairway to the kitchen, or if not, we will look under the steps to the outside doorway. Before he brought the box up to show you, did you hear any pounding or tapping? Did you hear anything when he carried it back down?"

"No. I could be wrong about what happened before he came up, but I was aware of everything after our talk about the box and what to do with what was in it."

"Then we need to look for it. Right?" They began by just lifting up the horizontal edges of the steps; none of them moved or seemed to have been disturbed lately. Then John tried the upright risers behind each step, and the second one from the bottom gave a little. Then he worked the riser slightly, and it came loose in his hand. When Amanda held the board, John reached down and came away with the metal box. He tried the lid, but it was locked.

Amanda said, "There is a little metal key with a string tied to it."

"All right! Then it is hanging on a nail close by, wouldn't you think?" And it was hanging from a nail on the inside of the plank steps.

When they checked to see if the packets of papers were still intact, John saw they were, and there was money under the bank shares. John asked Amanda if Mr. C. had told her how much he had set aside in the box to buy more banknotes. She studied a minute and then said, "He never mentioned there was money in the box.

"He told me, when we were going to buy Christmas presents, that I had not paid myself any salary, so I had money for presents. When I reminded him he had not paid himself either, he said he did, occasionally, when he needed money for the little box."

Remembering the trip to Greenville to buy presents brought a smile to her face. John saw it and knew she had loved the man and the life he had given her. He felt uneasiness, but he reminded himself there were many kinds of love, and he was glad this girl had finally found enough affection to know what love was. He doubted she had found any, of any kind, while she was growing up, and that must have been terrible. C. H. Connor had been worth a lot to many people, but personally speaking, John believed the gift of love, respect, and a future to Amanda was his greatest gift of all.

Upstairs in the clean, bright kitchen, Amanda felt warmer and safer than she had in a while. She told John how very much she appreciated his help in finding the box and braving the spooky, cavernous basement with her.

He said, "No problem, I want you to feel free to call on me anytime you need me. Dad feels the same way, and between us and Miles, we intend to keep you and this household safe." And he wondered again why he had not seen this girl's beauty until now. It was not that she wore better clothes now. Her dresses were still plain, and always before, she and her clothes had been clean and neat. There was something in her carriage, something in her expression that was so clear, saying she was not intimidated, and her eyes, oh Lord, those eyes could hold him spellbound.

"Maybe we should call the sheriff now in case Boyd or somebody is out there," she worried.

"Ben's been out there, knows where I am, and anybody who might want to harm me...or you." So he took his hat from the peg in the kitchen where he had hung it, and said, "Amanda, don't try to do anything alone. It would do my heart good to catch that mean little Chalmers boy doing something wrong. I think I could give him some discipline he has never had, and enjoy it to the fullest." So saying, his hand almost went out to touch her, but instead he flipped the kitchen light out, slipped out the back door, and melted away in the darkness.

Then she checked all the outside doors in the house and went upstairs to prepare for bed. In her prayers that night, she asked for protection for herself, for the Barretts, for John, for his dad, and for guidance for Ben Miles, who had the job, which was not an enviable task, of keeping the whole area safe. Then she asked for guidance for herself in the endeavors to do something for the wanting, hungry people. She asked for help to do the work Mr. C. had seen the need for and asked her to continue with. She asked that these people would accept her in this town and countryside. With that done, she slipped away into a healing sleep.

When daylight came, she waited to start a new day, and for the first time since Mr. C. had left her, she felt capably able and almost free of fear.

Chapter 6

The store was open when Amanda went in. Thomas had a customer, and everything seemed to be going along as well as it always did. When Thomas finished with his sale, he came to stand in front of her and said, "I have a proposition for you. What would it be like for me to come in early each day, open up, and go home early enough to do some farming? I know you don't want to be left alone to close up after dark. It will stay daylight longer as the days get longer, and soon you'll be getting home way before dark."

"I think that might work in a week or two, and right now, I will be needing to tend to some business away from the store at various times. If you will be available at those times, I would appreciate it and be happy for you to go home earlier." And she smiled.

"You know I will be glad to do anything I can, Mrs. C." And all of a sudden, he ducked his head, and his face was as red as a beet, and he said, "I am sorry, Mrs. Connor."

Amanda laughed and said, "Don't be sorry. I love to be Mrs. C. Bubba started it as soon as he realized I belonged with Mr. C., and I know both of you call me that when I'm not around. So feel free to call me Mrs. C., as it is much better than Mrs. Connor, and I can't stand Mrs. Amanda. I am still young, and as long as you respect me, I feel free to be Mrs. C. or just Amanda."

So the days started a little later for Amanda, and soon she closed at the same hour but got to the house before dark.

Then, one evening, the truck deliverymen from Dallas, with her grocery order, called and said they were broken down halfway between the wholesale house and Canesville. They asked if they could be an hour later getting to the store.

She hated that this was her only option, but she could not send them back to Dallas so they would have to make another trip the next day. So…she said "yes" in a very small voice.

The closer darkness came, the more squeamish she felt. She went to the phone twice to call John or Miles to let them know she was stuck at the store.

Then the truck pulled in. Amanda hurried to open the double back doors to the loading ramp. It did not take the boys long to put the order inside; then they jumped into the truck and headed on the long way back to Dallas. She hurriedly set the two-by-four back across the doors and promised herself there was no way she would go back behind the building to set the lock on the chain there for double safety. The question arose in her mind of why she had not had the delivery boys stay until she could get to her car and drive home, and that made her furious at herself.

She made an effort to start from the front door. Amanda looked down the alley to her car and started toward it, but something caused her to stop. She eased back through the door, reset the lock, set her bag down, and sat on the stool behind the counter.

"Well, this is what John told me to do. The locks have been changed, and this place is probably safer than the house," she reassured herself, trying to throw aside her unease and feel safe, and she did feel a little that way.

But soon she became restless and picked up the phone and told Beatrice Clemmons to ring John's number for her. Beatrice did and let it ring four or five times. Then she said, "Amanda, I think John and his dad are tied up in Clarksville in a court hearing. Is there anyone else I can try for you?"

Then Amanda said, "Thank you, I think not." So she went to the back of the store and pulled Mr. C.'s cot out and got ready to lie down for a while. The phone rang, and chill bumps on her arm made more and bigger chill bumps as she sat petrified. After the sixth or seventh ring, she finally took down the receiver, and her voice squeaked as she said a timid "Hello?"

"Amanda, are you all right?" It was Ben Miles, and she was so glad to hear a friendly voice she almost laughed in his ear.

"Yes, I am fine now. I was almost paralyzed thinking this call could be from some others."

Ben said, "What are you doing still at the store?"

"My delivery truck had trouble on the way down from Dallas and called to ask if they could come in late. They just left a few minutes ago."

"Oh...OK! I'll drive by in a few minutes; you lock up and I'll follow you home." So that time she got by with a little luck and wondered how Miles had known she needed him. She found out later Beatrice had called him when Amanda had not done it herself. From that time on, she lost all uneasiness about the telephone when Beatrice Clemmons was on duty and on the line.

A few days later, Amanda crossed over to Minningers to pick up a sandwich for her lunch, and she sat on a stool at the counter to wait for her food. She was busy trying to work out in her mind how she was going to approach the people who needed some of Mr. C.'s money instead of their bank shares. Then she resurfaced in the present, and all of a sudden, the hair on the back of her neck stood up, and a shiver ran up her arms. She realized a couple of boys had entered, and she knew who they were. Boyd Chalmers and his sidekick, Marvin Jones. She kept her eyes straight ahead and glanced to the back, behind the half partition between the counter and the kitchen, hoping Cleeb Moss was bringing her sandwich to the front. She did not see him coming forward. Then she heard Marvin Jones giggle, and he said, "Well, there she is, Boyd…free for the taking."

Then Boyd said, "Nah, I wouldn't touch her with a ten-foot pole since 'Old Wimpy Dick' had had her." And they both snickered and started laughing.

Then Cleeb was there with her sandwich; she quickly paid him and left. She made herself walk at the same gait she always did, even though all her nerves were screaming for her to run, to go faster and faster. When she was in the store, she felt awful. She felt sick at her stomach; the smell from the sack with her sandwich was making her feel she might throw up.

She left the sack on the counter and hurried to the bathroom, wet a towel, and bathed her forehead and then her throat. She sat for a while, and when the sickness was under control, she opened the door and started back to the front.

Then Thomas said, "Is there something wrong, Mrs. C.?"

And then she stopped and said, "Yes, Thomas, there is something very wrong, and I have to tell you about it. Do you know Boyd Chalmers?"

Thomas said, "Yes, I know him. The idiot with the car, everybody knows him. Is he causing you trouble again? I wish he would do it when I'm around, as I would dearly love to wipe up the ground with him."

Amanda felt well enough then to laugh a little, and she said, "Take a place in line behind John Halsey, as he would like to do the same thing."

Then Thomas said, "I really should resign and let you hire somebody full-time, as I know you hate to be by yourself late in the evenings."

"No way, Thomas. Don't even think about it. You are the only person I can leave this store with and not worry about a thing. If it comes to that, I can hire a person part-time and let him stay until I am on my way home."

* * * * *

A few days later, Holmes Carter called and asked if she had found C. H.'s shares, and she told him she thought so, that she wasn't sure. One white lie wasn't bad when it was told to an ungodly person.

Then he said, "I thought you were going to run them over here when you located them."

"Well," she said, "I have not been sure of whether they are all here, so I have decided to bring them to a board meeting so we can check them out."

"Now, Amanda, you don't want to get mixed up in all the folde-rol of a board meeting. You'll find it boring, and you know we are going to do everything right. I hear your business is doing well. I suggest you stay over there and see to it. Let us men take care of the banking. Right?"

She waited a moment and said, "No, sir. I feel Mr. C. wanted me to learn as much as I possibly could about all of his business; he may have told me some things to do he had not explained to the board."

"Now, Amanda, if you mean those little personal loans he made using bank shares for collateral, that was all foolishness. In fact, it wasn't really ethical. He was a member of the board, a shareholder, and those little trades he made were against all banking procedures. We should have called in all his shares, and that would have unseat-ed him from the board. So you are looking trouble in the eye by being obstinate about this. We intend to buy his shares. They are not worth a lot right now, but a least it will give you some working capital for your store."

"Mr. Carter, thank you for calling, and we will see how it goes." She hung up and looked upward and said, "Mr. C., how did I do? Without your training I would have caved in. And *Lord*, without *Your* help, I would not have the faith in my two fine lawyers and a sheriff fair enough to see justice done."

She felt Mr. C. was close enough for her to be able to say, "I love you so much." And she knew she did feel his presence.

Soon after the call from the bank president, he came over to the store. There was nobody there with her, and all of a sudden, she be-came afraid. She went behind the cash register and faced him across the counter, hoping her hands would not shake and her voice would work when she needed it. It was apparent he was still in his "good old boy" mood, because he had a warm, wide smile on his face and quick, jaunty steps that brought him across the counter from her.

"Hi," he said. "I don't think you understood what I was saying when we were on the phone. I didn't mean to be grumpy and dictatorial with you, and then I realized I should not have said anything negative about C. H. Of course, he is your knight in shining armor, and he should be. He took you out of a terrible life, with no hope of a future, and gave you more than you ever thought to have. He made you a lady, and I think you should be proud of the way you have handled yourself. Hell, this whole town is proud of you. All those folks that showed up when C. H. died were not there just because of him. They were there for you too. Some of us were paying respect to you as his wife."

He stopped and waited for her to thank him for his shallow, effusive accolades. She looked at him and found her voice. "Mr. Carter, I don't know what you are hoping to gain by this visit in person and your beautiful eulogy for me, but I am determined to finish Mr. C.'s business the way he wanted it done." And she turned, picked up her keys, and let him know she was through with this visit.

But he was not finished. He said, "Amanda, if you are going at this whole thing along with the Halseys, just remember one thing: they are lawyers. Lawyers always work to get as much money as possible for themselves. They would not worry about you or your business. You better watch out, or they will have the whole ball of wax, and you will have nothing."

"Thank you, Mr. Carter, have a nice evening." He finally spun around and went out the door. She turned around and said, "Thank you again, Lord." And then she giggled and said, "Thank you too, Mrs. Chaney."

Mrs. Chaney was a little old lady who still lived in the Olde English World she was brought up in. She was very adept at saying any criticism and/or disagreement in such a genteel way no one could take exceptions to her. She always knew what to say and how to say it.

When Amanda got home, the Barretts were ready to go across the patch to their little house. Bubba said they were going to plant some beans and corn, and from his enthusiasm, you would think the seeds were going to grow diamonds and pearls.

He said, "Mrs. C., when we have beans and corn, we will eat them at your house so you will have them too. OK?" And of course, she also said "OK." That was the way Bubba looked at life, especially nature. The wonder in his eyes brightened Amanda's life many times when he was amazed at the beauty and bounty of the earth and all that was in it.

She had wondered many times lately how she could face her existence without her lovely home to look forward to when her day of labor was done, and the two people who were actually the only family she had. She did wonder at times if her mother and father ever thought about her. Amanda remembered in her prayers to ask for blessings for them, and understanding and forgiveness for them in her heart and her life.

She realized she had been staying in the store many long hours of the day, and then, when she got home, she closed her doors and put the locks on them. Now she was determined she was going to go to the garden, and if there was no implement for her to use, she would just stay out there and visit. This was the right place to think about the chores Mr. C. had given her to do. She needed to find the right people to begin Mr. C.'s philanthropy—to start making a difference in some lives.

Then she got caught up again in her good life and knew without the Barretts, a clean, bright home, and nourishing food to come home to, her life would be harsh and empty. This she told Mary Barrett, and for the first time, she saw tears in that lady's eyes.

* * * * *

The days in the store went by quickly. It was the nights she found haunting, and sometimes she felt uncertain and fearful. She was doing her best to be a businessperson and was just managing to keep the store bookkeeping in the black. That was when she started keeping a little money salted away for the future. John had told her how much was in the box. Amanda thought maybe she would feel a little more secure with some unaccounted-for money stashed back. She wondered where in the world to put it and decided to use Mr. C.'s hiding place for her cigar box and the few dollars she could save for it.

Then her plans began to firm up, and she asked Mrs. Barrett for help. She explained to her what Mr. C. had been doing and told her that he had wanted her to continue on with his plans. She said, "Mrs. Barrett, you know you and Bubba are my family, and I need help on this. I am not tuned in and aware of the families in need as you are, and I need some help on how to start out.

"You know just about everybody and which folks are destitute and which are already on 'relief.' He said those on relief would get by. Those who have always been independent and trying to do for themselves are the ones Mr. C. was looking out for. Do you think you could check around and find some good but needy folks for me?"

"Goodness, Amanda, I don't have to check around. Paula Barnes said at church last Sunday that Jimmy is going to let her and their youn'un starve to death because he is too proud to ask for government help. She is expecting again really soon, and that child of theirs is not two years old. I'd say just look around you. They are right in front of our eyes." Amanda loved the pronoun "our" and saw now Mrs. Barrett was a member of Mr. C.'s benevolent dream.

Then Amanda asked her to make a list as time passed, and she would look at the list when she had found a way to help the Barnes family.

The next morning Amanda went in fairly early and helped Thomas set up the store for business. Then she gathered up a beautiful baby blanket and went to the Barnes farm. The road was wet, and she was not the best driver on slick dirt roads. She managed to get up the last hill before she got to the Barnes house.

She went in and played with their baby, who was so clean and smelled so sweet. She had known Jimmy would be in the house, as it had rained the night before, and it was past chore time.

Paula was excited about the blanket, but Amanda could see her counting what very needed things she could have bought with the cost of the frilly blanket. Amanda had picked the showy blanket for that reason; she did not come out here to show she knew this family was needy.

"Well," she said. "How are you folks making it out here? They are trying to say, in the newspapers and on the radio, the economy has bottomed out. What do you think?"

"Lady, whatta you think we think? This country has gone to hell and back. Now they are telling us how much cotton we can plant and are going to measure it to be sure of our allotted acreage. They want to be sure we can't plant a big enough cash crop to take us through another winter. There is no way to survive." And his bitterness was heartbreaking. "It looks like I'm going to sell my one and only cow that isn't mortgaged to buy enough staples to last till 'pea time.'"

Then Amanda saw a ready-made opening and asked, "Jimmy, maybe I could underwrite you through this time and maybe even pay off some of your banknote?"

She saw Paula's face light up, and then she looked at Jimmy and saw defeat there. He said, "How in the world would I ever pay you back? I'm behind at the bank, and that son of a _____ Carter is just waiting for an excuse to foreclose, so that he takes everything I have to work with—my mules and plow tools." He did not use blanks for what he called Holmes Carter.

"OK," she said. "Let me think a minute. I know Mr. C. was thinking the bank was being way too insensitive under Carter and was hoping to find enough supporters to oust him. In fact, I don't think he lacked many shares to have enough to give himself controlling interest."

"I would be glad to see the SOB get his just desserts, and if my paltry little shares would hurry it along, you are welcome to them." She saw the Jimmy was willing to help even if he got nothing.

"Wait a minute." She said. "Let me explain how Mr. C. handled the deals he made. He made a loan for enough to pay off the bank (or to pay up on the banknotes—enough to stop foreclosure), holding shares as collateral. He hoped that by having control of enough shares, it would hurry the housecleaning and settling the bank's business in capable hands. He never intended to keep the shares. He was simply holding them to secure the loans and make sure he had enough shares to force Carter out."

"You don't know how much we appreciate what you are trying to do. Even if you can't afford to do it, we are so glad somebody is trying. You really are a saint."

Then Paula burst into tears, and Amanda walked over, put both arms around her, and held her while she wept.

Amanda said, "Wait a minute, folks. Before you canonize me, let me tell you this is all Mr. C.'s dream. He was trying to do as much as he could while he was alive, and he gave me the plan, the power, and the means to carry on." "Now then, Jimmy, put pencil and paper to the banknote and enough cash to get you through until 'pea time.'"

"Pea time" in Northeast Texas, during those stringent times, meant when the gardens were in and there were green vegetables, including peas, beans, and potatoes, to refill the root cellar. There would be enough onions, radishes, and all kinds of greens to make a balanced meal, usually. White or Irish potatoes came in the early spring. Yams or sweet potatoes filled the root cellar in late summer. This bounty would get the family through the time when no cash crop was ready to be harvested. Most families made sure those things were grown, ready for canning and storing and the table, or for the market along with eggs, chickens, milk, butter, and cream.

Jimmy was trying to give his need a fair expression of his last year's crop when he and pregnant Paula had to pick their cotton, because if he had hired pickers to bring his crop in, it would have cost more than the finished bales would have sold for on the market.

In fact, when the government bought cows, they never paid enough to settle any banknote. Most of the loans had listed cattle at about thirty to fifty dollars a head, and the government was paying from six to ten dollars per cow.

Some of the men had gone to some of the "killing cows days" and did not believe they were not allowed to take meat home to a hungry family. It had been whispered that at some of the places of slaughter, a few of the government agents had stayed for the killing. Then the agents had stood, read the rules aloud, and left, leaving all the questions of right and wrong to every man's discretion and conscience.

What *was* right anymore? Amanda was not sure at all now. One thing she did believe, with all her heart, was that Mr. C. had been right. He had been right in what he had done and what he had planned. He had been right in what he had meant for her to do. She was very determined to do all she could, not just for Mr. C., *not* just for the privileged, but also for all the young families she visited who were eager to help her gather shares, even if there was no money for their needs.

She would help them stay together and save their families if she could. She knew a few of the young men had gone to the city and to far West Texas hunting jobs. That had caused rifts in the families and unhappiness between the couples.

When Jimmy had finished his list of the absolute necessities for the family to survive, plus the banknote, he left the room and came back. He opened a little metal box and took out his few shares and handed them to Amanda.

"Now then, Jimmy, you will need to saunter by the Halseys' office and sign a paper so I can use your shares to further tip the scales in the battle of right. When you pay off that banknote, you might hint some relative has seen fit to help you. Say whatever you're comfortable with." She looked at the face he had on at that minute and said, "I know what you would love to tell him, but we are not there yet. Don't mess it up. Easy does it until we get most of the folks around here with something to eat and other items they must have. By the way, who do you think should be next on my list?"

And Paula said, without a second of hesitation, "The Barkleys. They are planning for Will to go to Dallas or somewhere to get a job, and Nina would be left with two babies and all the work. Then there is her invalid mother to care for."

So Mr. C.'s project of mercy began anew.

*****

Amanda went to bed every night with a prayer on her lips that her money would hold out to see as many as possible in better circumstances; that she could keep the wolf, a very hungry wolf, from doors where a lot of young couples dreaded it with a true and honest fear.

Her money would have lasted a little longer if Paula Barnes had not had trouble having her baby. Jimmy asked for help so Dr. Story could go out and deliver the baby boy. Of course, she gave him the money and wondered how she was going to pay her restocking bills at the store the next time she ordered from the wholesale house in Dallas. She knew she must keep her credit rating up, or she might as well close her doors.

Then the Lord provided some help when Dr. Story paid her a call to give his fee from Jimmy Barnes to her as he said, "Do you not think I might make people feel better if we are helping what my good friend started? C. H.'s benevolent attitude has meant a lot more than a baby delivery fee." Then she wept a bit and hugged the doctor, whom she had resented at one time. When she went to bed that night, she knew not only that politics made strange bedfellows but also that any dedicated movement brought people and their efforts together.

Chapter 7

Amanda sat with her bookkeeping journal open and her bank statement in front of her one evening, and it became apparent she had to have some funds besides her little stack she had in the little box under the steps in the basement.

She had thought her bank account was more stable than it was, so there went her little cache in the hiding place. Her eye caught the gleam of her heavy ring on her finger, and she held it up to the light. She really looked at it for the first time since Mr. C. had put it on her hand nearly a year ago. Then she wondered where Mr. C.'s ring was. Did they bury it with him, or what happened to it? She remembered that Mr. Saunders had given her a large envelope at the cemetery and said, "I think you might need and want these personal things."

"But what did I do with them?" she wondered aloud. That all seemed like a dream now. She did not have any idea what happened back then and where she had put those papers.

She decided she would look for them when she got home. Mr. C. had said the rings were a good investment and that was what she needed now—a good, strong investment.

So saying, she took her keys, let herself out the front door, and was almost to her car when she heard steps behind her. She did not look back. She had the door opened and was in, almost to where she could close the door, when she felt fingers grab her upper arm. She saw the evil, grinning face and smelled the rotgut whiskey that would bring back memories of this awful boy as long as she lived. She punched the key in the slot and heard the quiet purr of the powerful motor as she moved the gearshift. She put it in reverse and gunned it, put on the brake, then shifted to forward gear and felt the grip of his fingers loosen from her upper arm. Then she very quietly eased forward. She knew the boy was on the ground, and she pulled along beside his body out of the lot.

When she got home, she called Beatrice and asked for Miles's office. The phone rang several times, but nobody answered. Then Beatrice asked, "Amanda, is there something wrong? I think Ben took a prisoner to Terrell this afternoon, but he should be back at any time now. He had hired a deputy, who should be on duty, but he may have gone home or to Minningers to eat supper or for coffee. Would you like for me to call around and see?"

"No," Amanda said. "If you hear from Ben, just tell him I need to talk to him. OK?"

"Sure thing." And Beatrice disconnected them. Amanda sat in a cold sweat until her phone rang, and she forced herself to take it down and say "Hello."

It was Ben, and he said, "Has something else happened, Amanda?"

Then she said, "Yes, and we need to talk. But first go by the parking lot where I usually park and see if there's somebody hurt there."

"Oh, hell, he did try to hurt you, again. Right?"

And she said, "Yes, he did. But he may be hurt and needing help. Would you go see?" And of course, he drove by and found the lot empty and wished, in a way, Boyd Chalmers was still there, lying in the dirt, hurting. This case of this spoiled, rotten son of a man with a government job was getting completely out of hand. Ben found himself questioning his ability to handle the situation of this boy's attacks in a fair and equitable manner. He knew he must keep Amanda safe and still not handle the situation improperly, for then the whole area would be in trouble. The kid was so thoroughly evil and rotten; he wondered how decent people could put up with him.

When Ben came to Amanda, she was fairly calm, he thought, but he saw her holding her arm and could see a bruise there.

"How is your arm, Amanda? And you must be pretty charmed as a driver to have jarred him loose. I don't want you to have to do these things alone, but of course, you had no peace officer on hand to help. I'm so sorry about that. You just keep on being C. H.'s angel of mercy. Don't think you are still in this alone. I hear the ladies of C. H.'s church are planning a box supper, and all proceeds will be used the way he was, and you are, doing the helping bit."

"My arm is fine. I think the adrenaline helped me not feel what my arm was going through. I had not felt anything until now." Then Amanda felt her heart fill with something—a growth so young and tender she had to recognize it as love. Not only had she loved, but also, now the love was coming from others—Mr. C.'s church and his friends. Once started, she intended to fill her life with it.

When Ben left, she felt warm and protected, cared for, and she stayed outside to listen to the night birds and frogs; then she heard a whip-poor-will. When she heard it, it made her think of her daddy. She remembered he said when he heard the first whip-poor-will, he knew it was time to plant cotton. She wondered if he had planted cotton this year, and if he did, he evidently had not shot the government agents when they came to measure it. She hoped he had learned some lessons of accepting things he could not change, that in some way he had feelings for others with their distresses. The fact that life had been hard for him was no different from what had happened to others during these trying and awful times.

She wondered if her mother could have been a little more open and pleasant, and she wished her father could have been a little more forgiving and thoughtful.

When she went inside, she felt somewhat relaxed and began to understand she had been entirely too close to her fear and dread. She had shut her house up so early every evening, and so completely, that she had felt like a prisoner in her lovely home. It was time to begin to live again, and she realized her one-woman crusade was to be a whole community affair. With the help of many, Mr. C.'s dreams would be realized. The thing with Boyd Chalmers was going to be taken care of by the nice men she knew. All she had to do was stay out of his way.

* * * * *

One Friday afternoon, she left Thomas and the store and took her wedding ring and Mr. C.'s heavy gold band to the jewelry store in Greenville. When she told the man they had bought the rings from she needed to have him repurchase them or lend her money with the rings as collateral, he seemed interested. He took them from her and set his lens gadget on each in turn; she watched him lay them down in front of him on the counter.

Then he asked, "Mrs. Connor, how much money do you need?"

She said, "Well, I think I need, or can get by with, seventy-five or a hundred dollars. We did pay that much for the rings, or more. Didn't we?"

"Yes, you did, but your ring has seen a lot of wear." And he smiled. "You haven't had it off much since Christmas. Right?" And he said, "When did you lose Herbert?"

"March 15. He wore his constantly until then, and I really thought it was buried with him. Then I remembered he said they would be a good investment. I found the ring in some papers and other things the undertaker gave me at the cemetery. It does look brand new, doesn't it?"

"Yes, it does. I think I can keep it for a while and let you have the money on it. You can redeem it anytime in the next year, or if you decide you don't need it, I can probably sell it for you." Then he looked at her and added,

"I keep hearing stories coming out of your little town about some lending of money with bank shares as collateral, and I think someone is doing a great service in your little community and county. You see, Herbert and I were friends. We went to Normal School together, and I was always interested in him and his little community. He always had a project going, and the one you are involved in is the best one yet. I hear the president of the bank is looking for a job in a larger town, and the latest rumor is he has found one in Dallas. Have your heard that?" He waited for an answer.

"No, I haven't heard that, but it would be wonderful if it is true. There is so much bitterness and hatred in our town and county, it would be a blessing if it would all end up as you have just said. It would be almost a fairy-tale ending, but I really don't think Carter will give up that easily."

"Oh, I think he will. Someone has leaked some information; one shareholder has 51 percent of the shares, so I think he will quit while he is ahead. He knows the movers and shakers are lining up staunchly behind the biggest shareholder, and he can get out now or go down in disgrace. Has nobody told you, you don't have to do everything by yourself?" And he looked her in the eye and smiled.

"Well, I have felt the wonderful backing of many of the folks who trade with me, and business has been so great that this order I am placing today is larger than usual. Everyone has bought everything to the bare walls. I didn't have time to check my accounts to find a net amount, so I just decided to call in a whopping big order and restock all that I'm low on. But…my bank statement says I am low on working capital…"

"Then I know more about your business than you do." And the dear man smiled again. "You see, your Mr. C. and I were pretty close friends, as I said, so I am interested in what is happening. He was always ready to talk to me about his town and his plans—his dreams. It seems there have been some errors in the bookkeeping at the bank, and I think your account is well and healthy now that the books balance again. I insist you take the hundred dollars with you and leave C. H.'s ring, which will put him back squarely in the very midst of his plan to help as many people as he could. It was his one-man crusade to help families face these terrible times, business-wise, to say the least."

Amanda laughed and said, "That would please my wonderful Mr. C., and he would cherish the whole idea of what had been done and what is ahead for our little community."

She left to go home with a warm and grateful feeling. When she got to the store, she sent Thomas home to do some late garden plowing. She sat down to make her order out and call it in to the wholesale house. She kept her feeling of well-being until she was finished with the order and noticed it was getting dark outside. She still felt a wonderful sense of achievement as she locked the door and started around to the place in the parking lot where she had left the car when she had driven it in from Greenville.

It looked unlevel for some reason, and before she got to it, she realized her tires on the right-hand side were both flat.

That was when she realized she was in trouble...real trouble. Somewhere out there was Boyd Chalmers. He was waiting, and the only hope she had was to outrun him. And that was when she took to her heels. She did not continue on to the car; she just cut through the parking lot to her street.

She was within a block of her house when she heard his footsteps and his panting breath behind her and knew he was going to catch her. That he would pull her to the ground and beat her senseless; she hoped he would beat her senseless before he abused her and raped her. She felt his hot breath and was attuned to his body as he gathered his muscles to propel himself forward and knock her off her feet. She heard his mouth spewing curses and evil threats when he lunged to stop her pounding heels. "Oh, God, oh God, help me now!" She wept. He made the dive toward her, but he never got there.

For some reason he had started, but his body had stopped and gone backward, and she had heard a dull thud as the breath left her attacker's lungs. She had caught a glimpse of some object that had gone by her head out of the corner of her eye. She had heard something besides the breath as it left Boyd's body.

Then she heard a snuffling sound and realized the blob that had gone past her side vision had come down from the limb of the hackberry tree that hung over the sidewalk.

Then she knew, without a doubt, the blob had been her salvation. The other sound, the dull thud, sounded like bone had connected with rock or concrete and was so sickening she was paralyzed with fear. She turned and saw Boyd on the ground, sprawled on his back, motionless, and it was plain something had hit him in the chest as he had made his leap forward. Something had come down from the huge tree limb.

She had heard something familiar yet strange. The she said, "Bubba, is that you?" And she heard the snuffle again, but there was no answer. She said, "Go home and don't talk to anybody. Just go home and know I won't be hurt anymore. I have to get help for Boyd and get Ben to take care of things. OK?" And she heard his shuffling gait pass across her backyard, and she prayed he would be cared for as all children should be.

She unlocked her door, went straight to the phone, and asked Beatrice to ring Ben for her. It was only a few minutes until the sheriff's car pulled into her driveway, and she met him there. Ben came straight to her and held her for a second, and then they walked across her drive to where Boyd was still stretched out on his back. With Ben's flashlight, they saw the lower back part of his skull was crushed on a loose slab of cement. Ben looked at the limb above that part of the walk and made a sound as if he were pleased things had happened as he figured they had.

"Where is your car, Amanda?"

"It is at the store with two tires slashed. He made sure I wasn't going to get away this time. But I did outrun him for a while. When he fell, he had just made a lunge for my feet, and he would have had them." She gulped and prayed the tears would not start.

"Seems a good thing to have a guardian angel sometimes, especially when the one who is supposed to guard his citizens goes home for supper without checking the things he is supposed to. Right?"

"Now Ben, we will have none of that. I knew, when I saw my tires flat, I should have called you before I left the store. I learned this afternoon in Greenville that some things have been going on, and no friend or foe has seen fit to tell me about them. I wonder just when I would have been told. I wonder just exactly when I became excluded from news of the town."

"You were supposed to be clued in tomorrow night at the box supper. I find it hard to keep secrets right now though. I need to call Clem Saunders and get the trash off the street. Are you OK?"

"Yes, I am sorry things came to this, and I know Boyd had an evil little mind, but after all, he is somebody's child and is cared about. Isn't he?"

"Not that you would notice. He was furnished that damnable car and was allowed to run wild, and nobody knows how many other kids he influenced to turn out bad. Anyway, it's out of our hands now. I have talked to him and his daddy lately and warned them to put a stop to this harassment, but they both thought it was funny. At least, they laughed."

So saying, he went in to use her phone to call Saunders, the undertaker, and she waited for him on the porch. When they had gone, Amanda went to the kitchen, poured herself a glass of tea, and finally ate some chicken and a biscuit.

Then she went over the day, incident by incident, held the wonderful people of this town and the surrounding areas to her heart, and asked that they could be blessed. She felt close to Mr. C. and wandered into his bedroom. She asked that he come closer and tell her what else she needed to do to finish up the work he had started.

It was quiet, very quiet, in this lovely room in this wonderful home that such a fair-minded man had made available to her. After all, she felt she was such a young, uneducated girl who had known so little about the business world and the people in it, and Mr. C. had changed that.

She let her heart and mind wander and knew the quietness that she was feeling was friendly. It was friendly because Mr. C. was here, and he always left people feeling blessed. Amanda felt he approved of her actions. Whatever good she had accomplished had come from him. She had only had him for a little while, but looking back, he had given her a message, a method to live by, and left her a woman with a promise and a purpose. She felt so young in years but so mature in her quest for a meaningful life. Mr. C. had given her a desire to learn and an eagerness for an education and for living with the world around her.

Some day she would study for a formal education, and until that time came, she would continue to learn as much as she possibly could. She would study many books, and the papers, but mostly the people around her. Someday, she hoped to find a man she would be happy to live with, and maybe she would even have a family. She really wanted to do that more than anything else.

Then she laughed and thought if she were grown enough, pretty enough, and educated enough, she knew a man who would be ideal and just right for the finish of all her daydreams. She remembered John, the handsome lawyer, with his insouciant grin and a touch that made her feel cared for and safe. But even when he took a place in her building of her air castles, there was also a trembling in her mind and body—a feeling that promised something ahead that was unknown. It made her afraid—scared, yet she felt it could develop into something wonderful and awe-inspiring. The only way she was ready for it now was in her fantasy world, and in that, she had no real knowledge, just feelings.

Maybe these feelings were akin to what her mother said made the Devil work in boys. Maybe it was wrong for her to have these new feelings. Did Satan work in women as well as in boys and men? She did not know. How could what she was feeling to be evil? It did not feel evil. It felt fine, with a promise of rightness that was close to… what? Pleasure? Yes. And it did not feel wrong.

Her faith was strong now, and she knew good things would happen to her if she did the best she could and kept the settling of others' problems foremost in her mind and heart. Some way, she hoped that someday she would be privileged to help others have a chance to fulfill their dreams, as Mr. C. had helped her. She hated that one of God's creatures had to die. She did not feel any guilt; she felt free for the first time in a long time, yet there was a little unease about how it had happened. Bubba was a child in a man's body, and she hoped and prayed this whole thing would not unsettle him and make him feel guilty. He had done what he had to do. She knew he had wanted to protect her because she had belonged to Mr. C. He had done a wonderful job of that protection.

Amanda was so busy the next day with her customers and her big order at the store; she had no time to worry about food for a box supper. Thomas was in the very middle of harvest, and she was doing more hours of work by herself.

When she got home, the boxes were filled, and all she had to do was wrap and decorate them. She had never been to a box supper and had no idea what the boxes should look like. Mrs. Barrett and Bubba told her their ideas, and finally, they were satisfied with her wrapping, and so was she.

When they got to the church, there were people, mostly men, standing around outside, and some of the men met them and offered help getting the boxes from the back seat. Bubba was hunkered there, and Amanda had seen Mrs. Barrett spread a tablecloth over the boxes. It was plain the Barretts knew what the men were up to, and Amanda did not have to wonder long. Paula Barnes met them at the door and congratulated them on getting the boxes inside with none of the men knowing what they looked like. It took a while for Amanda to realize the boys and men wanted to know which boxes were whose so they could outbid the husbands and boyfriends of the owners.

This was the first time Amanda had been to a social with a party atmosphere, and she was pleased to see the carefree attitude of the women and girls. They insisted Amanda be included in the guesses of which husbands and boyfriends had found out which box belonged to which lady.

Then Paula said, "I've got a sneaking suspicion John Halsey would like to know Amanda's box. Most likely he, and all the others, would be pleased with Mrs. Barrett's box too. Either hers or Amanda's will be a bargain because of Mrs. Barrett's cooking." Then

Amanda saw a different Mary Barrett as the lady's face lit up, and her smile was a work of art. Amanda was so happy to see her pleasure that she forgot to be embarrassed about what Paula had said, that John wanted Amanda's box.

That conviviality set the tone for the whole party. As Judge Halsey took the podium as auctioneer, the men showed no hesitation to bid on their wives' boxes and bid on other men's wives' or girlfriends' boxes, just to run the prices up. The place was so alive with good, solid friendship and cheerful banter that Amanda was flabbergasted at what she saw and heard. The men complained and promised retribution for the ones who bid against them for their wives' boxes, which they pretended they felt pressured to buy.

When the boxes were all sold, the ladies went looking for their suppers. If their husbands had somebody's box, not hers, then both couples sat down and shared. Everybody felt free to sample other food, and if someone had a new or different dish, the recipe was copied for others. It was a lovely time. Amanda wondered how much of her good feeling was for the company here, and how much was knowing she did not have to dread and look over her shoulder for Boyd Chalmers anymore. Nobody mentioned his demise, and neither did she. She felt she should not be feeling such carefree relief, but she could not dampen her carefree feeling and the escape from depression.

It was a lovely time, and the friends she had made at the store and through her offers of help were introducing her to their friends. She just sat and wondered why she had never known there were people like these in the world and that folks got together for a lot of fun and games.

When the food was eaten, the judge got up to tell just how this whole shindig was an effort to aid Amanda in her job of trying to loan money or pay out money with the bank shares as collateral. There was clapping, cheers, and some whistles.

"Without her and her late husband, times could have been worse for some of us. We salute you, Amanda Connor, and your wonderful Mr. C."

She could have crawled under a bench. Everybody was looking at her, and she was petrified. She did not want to speak, but she knew she had to answer those words. When she got to her feet, her legs were shaking, and she wondered if she even had a voice. She took the time to look into the faces of these wonderful people.

Then she said, "You are all winners, survivors. While this country has been in the depths of a depression, an economy so stagnant it made no sense to the people in power and certainly not to any of us, you survived.

"You made do with less. You gave up a lot of material things the affluent twenties made us believe were our rightful due. We all had to lower our standards of living. We may have grumbled, but nobody quit trying, and nobody is a failure until he or she quits trying.

"All that has been done through me was because I knew and loved a wonderful man. He left a legacy of caring and love for his fellow man. This, what we have done, was his project. He lived it and believed it, so let us take a little time here to remember him with the love he so richly deserves." And she sat down.

The hall was so quiet for a minute, and she thought it would be heard if a pin dropped.

Then Judge Halsey asked, "Isn't she a lovely lady?" Then the clapping began and got louder, and her tears began. She knew she was not the only one who felt the presence of a wonderful personage.

* * * * *

Amanda felt that with the help of other citizens and the money raised from the box supper, her life would be easier, and it was for a while. The smooth running of her business was a blessing after the bank's bookkeeping was back on track and she had enough working capital.

One day Amanda picked up her mail from the post office, and there was a very long, legal-looking envelope with a return address of a law firm in Houston, Texas. She wondered what lawyers in Houston had to say to her, so she sat on a stool behind the cash register, opened the envelope, and started to read.

When she began, even with the "legalese" in the letter, it told her Dermott Connor, a brother to C. H. Connor, was asking for a settlement of half the business of Connor Mercantile and the home of his parents. The letter said since the business had been founded and owned by the parents of Dermott and C. H. Connor, Mr. Dermott Connor felt, in all fairness, one half of the business belonged to him. He was also asking for a settlement of the homestead.

The old fears came back in control again, and Amanda was stiff and panic-stricken. All her hopes and dreams began to wither and die. She saw this threat as a way to lose everything, and the cost of all the hard work and plans became as flighty and without substance as her childish daydreams. Dreams she had as a country girl from the sticks—a foolish hope of entering high school and getting an education. The education was, she had realized, to come from a shortcut. When she could make her business pay and have people who could keep it running, she would take time to attend East Texas State Teachers College in Commerce, Texas.

She sat there for a long time, well past closing time, and could not find the strength to rise, lock up the door, and find her way home. She found she felt a strange inertia holding her in its power, and she became as listless as she had been the first weeks after Mr. C.'s death.

When she got home, the Barretts had gone, and she had absolutely nothing to do. She was not afraid now in the town itself, not on the street to her house, so she fixed herself a glass of tea and made her way to her room. When she walked to the window and looked out at the upper porch, she thought, "There is nobody here in our little town that wants to harm me now, so maybe it is time for me to crawl out on the deck and see the sights again."

This she did and found it a pleasant place. She went back inside, got a pillow and an afghan, and curled herself into a ball in a corner of the porch to think and wonder just what this brother had done to Mr. C. Just what could he have done to cause such a fair-minded and loving man to make him state, in his burial invoice, to only let one day pass before his funeral service? He had stated he wanted only his friends and church people in attendance.

She knew this was something she would have to see the Halseys about, and she became settled enough to believe she could sleep. Then she slipped back inside, brushed her hair, cleaned her face and teeth, and went to bed.

The next morning she felt gratified she had indeed slept, so she showered, dressed, and went down to breakfast. She did not tell

Mrs. Barrett about the letter, but she asked her if she had known Mr. C.'s brother, Dermott.

Mrs. Barrett looked as if she tasted something not just spoiled but purely rotten. Then she said, "Of course, I knew that no good crook. C. H. just got tired paying him out of trouble, so he set up a monthly retainer so that the only way the old boy could get the money was to never set foot in this town again. How do you know anything about him? He drew money C. H. let him have free, gratis, as he had already paid him handsomely for any share he could have claimed in the family business."

Mrs. Barrett never knew what a great relief her news about the derelict brother brought to Amanda when she told her the story. The story of why Mr. C. did not want his brother there for his funeral. What she wanted to know was how to go about finding out all these things. She hoped the Halseys knew what to do and how to answer the law firm's letter.

When Amanda got to the store that morning, Thomas had everything set up, so it was easy for her to sit down and write the questions she needed to ask the Halseys. When she felt their office was open for business, she called and asked if one of them could talk to her. The judge answered the phone, and he said, "Amanda, I could see you now, but I know John will be here in a few minutes. I am sure he had rather it be his job instead of mine."

Amanda said, "It wouldn't hurt for you both to see what I am into now. I had just begun to feel, at this time, I could relax a little and lead an uneventful life, as it was. Now up jumps another problem. Will it never end?"

When Amanda walked into the office, both men had a cup of coffee, and there was one waiting for her on a table by the divan.

She sat and passed the letter to the closest man, who was John. He looked at the letter and turned to his dad and said, "You win again. It is about Dermott, and he is asking for half of the business, again." He read the letter, then passed it to his father, who read it with his brow wrinkled and his lip pulled to one side.

The judge was quiet for a little time, and then he said, "I wasn't sure I knew what snake was trying to get his fangs into you, Amanda, but I had felt all along I knew a couple—a rattler and a sidewinder—who would try. I knew, at least, those two would make an effort to give you a problem. Their thinking would be that you might offer an out-of-court settlement rather than wait out a court proceeding. I am sorry, in a way, we didn't warn you and let you prepare for these things. Really, though, we wanted you to have a little time to relax and have a chance to live peacefully for a little while."

Then Hap Halsey said, "It reads about like I expected. In fact, we discussed this last week and were surprised he has waited this long to approach you for money any way he thought he might get it."

Amanda curled her fingers into her palms and tried to stop the trembling in her voice. "What can he get from us? What right does he have to demand half of what Mr. C. labored and built into a going business? If Mr. C. believed he was due anything, he would have given it to him gladly."

"He did that. He paid him not once, but twice," John said.

Then Amanda asked in a more settled voice, "Can we prove it?"

Then the judge said, "Indeed we can. Do you want us to send copies of C. H.'s checks, or do you want us to let them bring suit against you and let everybody know just how greedy Dermott is and how generous C. H. Connor was?"

"We don't have to prove anything about Mr. C. Just about everybody knows how he helped people all he could. A lot of us knew and loved him, and I think his brother must be the lowest scum to have taken everything he could and still be asking for more."

"You are very right. He is the very bottom of a cesspool." This was John speaking.

"But how did this happen? I asked Mr. C., soon after we went to Oklahoma, why he was so loving and giving with all people. He told me he came from the home of very deeply devout Christian parents, and he was taught from the beginning what a Christian family was supposed to be. How could his brother be a complete antithesis in every way to what the family taught and performed as a lifestyle and doctrine?"

"When one knows the whole story, it becomes a little clearer about the two men who never should have been raised as brothers. Dermott was born to a sister of C. H.'s mother. The sister died soon after Dermott was born. Some said she died from neglect and malnutrition. Later, when C. H.'s father checked on the brother-in-law, he found the child dying from the same kind of homelife that had ended the mother's life.

"He paid the brother-in-law a little money to sign a paper saying he could adopt the boy. He did adopt him, and he became, legally, C. H.'s brother. The family felt so sad he had lost his mother so young they overcompensated, so he grew up knowing he did not have to work or even conform to the rules of the family."

"Sometimes one wonders if there is really a bad seed," he added. "Anyway, the family was so sorrowful the child had grown so far with an abusive and neglectful parent in the midst of filth; too little was asked of him, and too little discipline was spent on him.

Even when he was small, he wanted everything C. H. had and was allowed to take it."

Amanda said, "Mr. C. told me about his parents, but he never mentioned his brother. Then, when Mr. Saunders was explaining about his funeral plans, he did tell me Mr. C. had a brother, and I asked how to contact him. Then he said we might be able to contact him, but Mr. C. had asked that only one full day should be observed before his funeral. He wanted to be put down with only his loved ones, friends, and church members in attendance. Now some things are beginning to make sense. I wondered why he had insisted he was to lie in state for only one day. He really wanted to be buried before his adopted brother could get here. Right?" she asked.

"Sounds right to me," the judge said. "Now let me explain to you just what C. H. had done to be rid of the man who was legally his brother. When he got the store going again, after the sicknesses and deaths of both parents, and was making some money, Dermott came here and just about moved into your Mr. C.'s home. No one knows where he had been, but he had no money, no clothes, and was filthy. It became apparent Mrs. Leona was afraid of him, so Mr. C. rented a room for him out of town at the Baxleys. That only helped part of the time, as he showed up at the store or at the Connor's house just about every day for something to eat.

"C. H. got him a job at the Martin's Grist Mill, and you can guess how long that lasted. Finally, after hearing constantly how disappointed Mama and Daddy would be that C. H. had taken over the business and he, Dermott, had never seen one dime from it, C. H. paid one half of a legal appraiser's assessment of the store and the home. C. H. wrote a stipulation that this was his last and final payment of any and all belongings of their parents, and

Dermott signed it. But C. H. made a mistake. He gave him all the money at one time. After a few years, the money was all gone, and here he was, back, ready for Mr. C. to feed him or give him money to buy food. And he still had to pay for a place for him to sleep, as by that time Mrs. Leona was terrified of him. When she had all she could stand of her home being invaded at any time, mostly when C. H. wasn't there, by a filthy, uncouth derelict, your Mr. C. knew he had to do something. He made a deal with Dermott to send him a stipend each month for enough money for him to eat on. He made him know that Dermott could only get the money if he never set foot in Canesville again. One trip here and the money would stop. Also, Ben Miles talked to him and let him know he had been lenient about Dermott coming in and out with no home or anything else. This, Ben promised, was over. He would pick him up as a vagrant, and he would serve time. That was what we were doing when C. H. died, and we have continued with it to now. Do you want us to continue sending the money so he doesn't come here? In a way, I wish he would show up, as the last deal they made would be nullified. It would free the rest of the money to go to others who are worthwhile citizens. Now, you go home and quit worrying about any of this. Dermott is sorry, but he is not a person to be dangerous. Right, John?"

And John looked at her and said, "The only danger that would worry me about being around him would be vermin."

Amanda shivered and rubbed her arms before she looked at John to see the devilment in his eyes and the half smile on his face. Then John said, "We will reply to this letter to these lawyers, explaining all that has happened so far in the brothers' lives. We will tell them we have proof Dermott was paid handsomely for any and all claims he could have as part of what used to be a family business. His deceased brother is also subsidizing enough money each month for food for him to eat. If there is still a question of whether he is owed more, we will send copies of what we have of proof of payment. Otherwise, they can bring charges, and we are prepared to meet them in court."

Amanda sat still in her chair and finally said, "I can't believe how long-suffering that wonderful man has been through the years. How would he believe such help should come from him over and over, even after his death?"

Then John said with a smile, "He did it all the time. His way of putting it was 'If we are to send aid to all the countries of the world, then surely we must feed the wanting and unfortunate ones here.' For some reason, I think he still felt something for the boy who had been abused and misused. You see, Dermott came to that family expecting nothing but abuse and tried every way he could to make the abuse continue. He felt that if he really belonged to the family, the abuse would happen. When it didn't, he felt he had drawn a blank. Does that make sense?" Amanda shook her head. He continued, "Not to normal people. We feel it would be a simple thing to cut him loose and let him face a bitter life. But we are not C. H. Connor. Dermott was not normal. He was all twisted from his early life, and we all know C. H. was so grateful for his own blessings in his life—he had to share. A good life with a Christian lady who loved and respected him, a fellowship with business associates, a prospering business and hosts of friends and fellow church members. His records show his life's work was the very living epitome of altruism. He lived an openly Christian life—a successful life."

Then Hap said, "Amanda, would you have us do anything different? Do you want us to stop the money we send him? You see he has broken the deal C. H. made him. By sending a threatening letter, which amounts to the same upheaval that his coming here to interrupt the business and your life would at this time. It constitutes the same thing."

Amanda sat for a long time, not moving, not speaking; then she said, "You know, I told Mr. C. I am not as good as he was, and I am not. I said that I didn't think nice things about people who did and said awful, hurtful words to me and about me. I wasn't forgiving about some things that had happened in my life. I am guilt-ridden, not so much about Boyd, for we all feel he was a threat to everybody, especially to young people. Yet I think some of these things happened to make me a stronger and more forgiving person. So I am not going to become a complaining, paranoid person, trying to pin on fate and God all my ups and downs. Do what has to be done. Don't stop the checks. Just mail them through the lawyers. Explain to them what our wonderful Mr. C. had worked out and that I am going to continue with the monthly stipend. Mr. C. started the plan for how best to care for the terrible brother, and I would not break the promise he made by stopping the checks. By the way, when the amount you have runs low, tell me, and I will put more in the kitty."

With that, she rose from the chair and said, "I know I can never measure up to that wonderful man who taught me so much, but I will never knowingly discontinue, or cut back, any projects he had in place." Then she shook hands with these gracious mentors who had, since Mr. C.'s death, been there to talk to her without forcing any ideas of their own into her decisions. When they needed her thoughts and opinions, they always gave her a least two options and waited for her to ponder what to do and how to do it. That had worked for them, as her decisions were based on what Mr. C. would do, or what he would want her to do.

She went back to work and felt fairly well satisfied. She felt burdened at times, yet she knew she would never wish the awesome changes in her life had not happened. She felt weak at times, and once in a while, she cried herself to sleep, but she felt Mr. C. up there. Wherever he was, he would not be unhappy with her decisions and work so far.

She felt small, young, and unsure of the decisions she had made to fill her life, not for just herself, but for others. Often, she went out on the rooftop outside her window with a pillow and a quilt, feasted on the beauty of the heavens, and communed with God. She felt safe here, free of the cares of the world, and found she could feel closer to Mr. C. up there, enjoying the heavens. If not closer to him, she knew she felt closer to God. She thought maybe she had the two of them mixed up, the same way Harold Bell Wright had portrayed the exceptional child in *The Shepherd of the Hills*. His father had found him as he roamed the Ozark Mountains, and to the boy, he became what he had been taught God was. He mixed his biological father with his Heavenly Father in his mind, and ordinary people did not understand. She could understand how it had happened in the mind of an exceptional child, for she could almost feel Mr. C. guiding her as an emissary of the Heavenly Being.

Maybe Bubba had a little of the unworldly reasoning. He had never mentioned the night Boyd had died on the sidewalk, just short of the Connor property line. He had never questioned who her attacker was, or why he was chasing her. He seemed satisfied he had not gotten involved, because somebody was trying to harm a person he felt was family. She wondered sometimes if Bubba had told his mother the part he had played in the happening. If he had, Mrs. Barrett never mentioned it and seemed satisfied with the report that the boy had died from a fall. She wondered if Bubba even knew his body slam had been fatal, because Boyd's name was never mentioned at all in the family. The question was never raised as to why the boy had fallen backward, and she was willing to let it go at that.

Chapter 8

Amanda found the strength to go with the days. She still felt she was a part of the town, and many of her customers had truly become her friends. The most important ones, besides the Barretts, were the Halseys. In their quiet way, they took care of her business and assured her everything was all right.

Then, one morning, John called the store and asked if she could come over for a confab about a matter. Of course, she said she could, so she washed her hands, since she had been handling yams, and went along to their office. Their office had become a place she prized, as it was where she came for help and reassurance. When she got there, she said, "What now?" And John said, "Trouble, and since this is the only time we see you, we think we should talk it through."

She said, "I am sure it is bad news, so let it out."

"Well, it could be bad news, or it could be classed as good news. It is strictly how you look at it. The lawyers in Houston have called and said one Dermott Connor has died and asked if we could forward enough money to pay for a burial," John said. "We didn't say one way or other. We told them we would talk to you and do whatever you decided."

"But John, how am I supposed to feel about a lout (as Mrs. Barrett called him) who felt that if one had something, one was sinning if they didn't share it with him?" Amanda's eyes flashed, and she bristled and then collapsed in a chair.

"Amanda, that is something you need to think on, and you don't have to make up your mind today. I don't think Dermott felt that way. He didn't know anything about sharing. He would have taken it all. C. H. was the one who thought, since he had so much, he should share."

Then Amanda raised those deep blue, almost purple eyes, with the darker rings around the pupils, and he saw they were glistening with tears. Once again, he felt that sharp pang around where his heart was supposed to be. He wondered how much longer he could last, letting this lovely girl grow toward maturity. He admitted to himself it wasn't just letting her mature; it was letting her work out her grief over her loss of the first person who had really loved her. Her love for the man would last her a lifetime, and he wanted it to; he just hoped she would realize there were different kinds of love.

This attraction for this girl had brought on unrest and uneasiness when he was supposed to be thinking of legal matters, and sometimes he was all involved in a daydream such as he had not experienced since his high school days. He realized she was carrying a heavy load while she should be going to school and parties, having dates, and living a very pleasurable time. Running a fully supplied business with only part-time help was time- and energy-consuming. Then there was her loan office job that many grown men would whine about. Men in the banking business found that job full of trials and errors, but he had stayed up nights checking those loans that she had made and was amazed at the names and amounts. She had put strict rules on herself that she had gone by to stop anything that was the least bit iffy. Sometimes he was puzzled at how she reasoned her actions, and he knew that the loans she had made depended on character and willingness to work. He found no bigotry or class (if there was such a thing) involved in any of her loans.

At times, he would be glad when her year of mourning was over and he could spend some time with her. He was not waiting to suit her or himself, but to show respect to a marvelous man and keep the respect the people here had for Amanda. He knew this was the right thing to do; however, sometimes his overworked fantasy took over, and he almost embarrassed himself. He wondered how much longer he could be satisfied being her attorney and her friend. The truth of the matter was, he wanted to be closer to her now.

He realized he had never been in love before, and he knew he was far too old for what was happening to him now. He would gaze into those unique eyes and would forget what he was saying. He wanted to worship her lovely body. He wanted to hold her and kiss her many, many times. He never had believed being in love could be so painful, both mentally and physically.

Through college and law school, he had dated many girls and ladies. He had been pleased with some of them and was proud to escort them to get-togethers, fraternity parties, and dramas around campus. He had never brought one home and had never felt any sorrow when they called a halt to their dating. They always did call a halt when they realized he was not ready for commitments. Each time they went their separate ways, usually they remained friends.

He had loved his life as a bachelor. He came and went as he pleased, except the judge usually knew about where he was. No woman had ever kept him awake nights, and no other had caused him to walk by a place of business just to catch a glimpse of her. He castigated himself for being like a teenager with hormones screaming in his blood.

Now he was scared out of his wits that he would make a mistake, come on to her too strong and lose any chance he might have to be looked on with genuine affection and trust. He remembered the night in her basement. He had looked at her and had become petrified. How could he lose his sanity just by being close to her? He did not know…Amanda said, "What I think about this is not what I need to do. You have made me see Mr. C. as a well-rounded businessman and the Christian I knew he was from the beginning. I am sure some of what happened with his unprincipled brother, who was actually a cousin, was because of Mrs. Leona. He may have gone further turning his other cheek had he not known his first priority was his wife. He loved her. So let's get busy doing what he would be doing if he had lived until this happened."

The smile on the faces of her counselors and friends made her see she was doing exactly what they had expected her to do.

Then John said, "Amanda, there is enough money in the account set aside for Dermott's little stipend to have him buried. We feel there would be too few mourners for a funeral, so we expect to cover the cost of some kind of casket and placing him under and a stone with his name on it. Now we will call the lawyer to ask the undertaker for the least amount for which he can get a grave site and some kind of stone for him. If there is any left in that account, we will add it to the funds in the little tin box." And he laughed, and so did Amanda. She thought even Dermott would have a share in Mr. C.'s philanthropy.

Even though the weather was bad for this part of the world, Amanda was busy and had a feeling of well-being she had not felt before. Time passed swiftly, and although Christmas had been another first without Mr. C., she felt the friends and the Barretts, those she treasured, had helped her get through it. She made a time to buy more reading material and a dress for her mother and a fleece-lined jacket for her dad. She still felt emptiness in the place she wished her parents were...in her heart.

* * * * *

Amanda had noticed a too grown-up but very young girl who came to town often in a wagon with her father. There was something about her that made Amanda stop and wonder why one so young was free to come to town on school days. It was plain she could not be eighteen years old, the approximate age for a high school graduate. She was bright, always seemed in a good humor, and could sense what her dad needed almost before he did. They always loaded out the wagon by middle of the afternoon, so she felt they had a long trip home. Also, they bought cheese and crackers, and usually some fruit, to eat on the way home.

One day, when the man and his daughter were in the store, she found Jessie—she now knew her name—looking through a book she was studying. When she glanced at the book, Jessie said, "I am sorry, Mrs. Connor," and laid the book down as if it were hot, as if she had done something wrong...Amanda said, "No, I am the one who is sorry. I would never object to anyone reading any book. I love them myself. Where do you go to school?"

"Well, I don't right now. I went to a little country school, Birdsview, across the river, close to our farm. I went as long as they would let me, because we can't afford for me to go to school here. A bus doesn't go back to our place to pick me up. We tried to think of a way for me to live in town, work for my room and board, and go to high school, but Daddy thinks everybody is as strapped for money as we are."

"Well, now, are you sure you are ready for high school?" Amanda questioned.

"My last teacher, Mrs. Riggs, let me repeat ninth grade twice and let me borrow as many books as she owned, and she could borrow for me. She said I learned so fast I probably could pass a college entrance exam with just my studies I've done since I left school."

Amanda studied her a bit, and then she said, "Let's talk to your dad and see if we can find a way for you to go to school, or for you to have the books you need to progress farther in your studies."

When Jessie Coats's father came to tell her it was time to start for home, Amanda said, "Mr. Coats, Jessie says you would be agreeable to her living in town and going to the high school here. That is, if she had a place to stay. Is that still an option?"

"Mrs. Connor, she is a straight-A student and has been since she started at six years old. My wife and I always thought she would be educated as far as we could possibly manage, but this Depression thing has torn into our plans. Mrs. Coats died year before last, and Jessie has taken her place with the cooking and laundry and still helps me with the farming. Before that happened, she was still able to study and try to learn as much as she possibly could. Now it is a struggle to keep food on the table and clothes on our backs."

Amanda looked him in the eye and said, "Mr. Coats, if I offered to let Jessie live with me and work some for her room and board, would you be able to do your work and eat without Jessie's help?"

"Oh, yes ma'am, I could. She doesn't have many clothes to wear, as she has about worn out the ones her mama made her. Her shoes are still pretty good, and she is healthy and as smart about work as she is about books."

"If she does housework and cooking, she is way ahead of me, and from what she has told me, she may be ahead in school work too. I plan to take the college entrance exam, and it may be fun to have someone else reading for the same goals I am. Why don't you both think about it this week and tell me what you think your next trip to town. If you want to do it, Jessie, just bring your things."

"You think about it, Mrs. Connor, and be sure you are not biting off more than you can chew," he said, and Jessie and her father crawled onto the wagon seat. He clucked at the team, and Amanda watched them leave. She was wondering if she could have, as Mr. Coats said, bitten off more than she could chew.

When she got home that evening, she found Mrs. Barrett and Bubba waiting to eat supper with her. They did that a lot even though they could go home whenever they chose and were never to stay past six o'clock. So the food was consumed, and then Amanda said, "I am considering doing something for a young girl, and I think, as you two are my family, you would be concerned more than anyone else.

"She is Jessica Coats, and they live too far away for a school bus to pick her up for school. Her father hasn't enough money to pay for her to board in town. She is a lovely girl, clean and very, very smart. She is so hungry for knowledge she repeated the ninth grade twice. Her teacher was so interested she let Jessica have books to study when she had to stay home and take over the housework, after her mother died. I think she can start in the middle of the term with no problem. Every child in Texas is due an education, and if Mr. Coats had pushed hard enough, I think something could have been worked out."

The Barretts sat quietly and listened while she told them about Jessica; then Mrs. Barrett said, "Will she be working in the store, or do you mean here?" And Amanda knew Mrs. Barrett was far ahead in the story, and she smiled.

"Mrs. Barrett, she can cook, clean and do laundry. She has been taking care of a household, and I can't begin to do what she is capable of doing. I have often wondered what we would do if you ever got sick. But that has nothing to do with what we can do for Jessie. She will be working at the store when she is not in school. I want it that way so maybe she and I can study together some. She will be willing to do Sunday morning breakfast and teach me to do Sunday dinner for the two of us and maybe have you and Bubba over to eat with us sometime."

Mrs. Barrett said, "I think I knew the Coats family back before times got so hard. They seemed to be respectable; both the parents used good English, seemed pleased with their little community and our little town. Mrs. Leona visited with Mrs. Coats at the store, and they discussed the quilts they had made, and I truly believe she was a lady." And with that said, Amanda knew she had Mrs. Barrett's approval in place to bring Jessie home to live with them.

She still felt she needed some time to think things through more thoroughly and to say a prayer for guidance. She must talk to the school superintendent. She knew this step was something that would have an influence and an impact on more people than just her household. And she did talk to Mr. C. D. McDougal, the superintendent of schools, and got an OK to start Jessica in the school system.

When the Coats father and daughter came to town the next Saturday, they were very quiet and came in as usual to fill their grocery bill. Then, as Amanda got finished with the customer she was with, she went over to where Jessica was standing and said, "What did you decide?"

And at the same time, Jessica said, "What did you decide?" They both laughed, and they both said "Yes" at the same time.

So Amanda and Jessica agreed to work together and study together. When they got home, Amanda said to Mrs. Barrett, "This is Jessica Coats." Then she said, "Jessica, this is Mrs. Barrett and Bubba. They are my family, and I think we can live together. Not just live, but enrich each other's lives."

The supper was a wonderful meat dish with vegetables around it to tempt any appetite. There was, as always, milk for Bubba and iced tea for Amanda and Mrs. Barrett. They gave Jessica her choice, and Mrs. Barrett seemed pleased when the girl chose milk. When supper was over, Jessica picked up the dishes and silverware and took them to the sink, and Amanda thought, "We shall see what we shall see." She was very pleased when Mrs. Barrett watched her fill the pan with water and add soap, and then Mrs. Barrett pointed to different cabinets and shelves for different dishes; then she put cold cream on her hands and said "Good night" and left.

Amanda sat in stupefaction and finally asked the world and the heavens, "Will wonders never cease?"

When Jessica was finished in the kitchen, Amanda took time to go with her upstairs to show her the bedroom she thought would be nice for her new guest. Well, she would not be a guest—nor just an employee; maybe at some time she would be a family member.

The first thing Jessica said as she opened her battered suitcase was "Mrs. Connor, I don't have many clothes, so Daddy gave me five dollars to buy something so you won't be ashamed of me." Her face was red, and her voice quivered.

Amanda looked at the two dresses that were well worn, but she could see they had been neatly made of good material. Then she said, "Jessica, when I came to this house, I had less. Mr. C. had to buy me a dress before I could go to church with him. You will never have to be ashamed around me about anything. I am so sorry you lost your mother at the time in your life when you needed her most. I lost mine at about the same age. She did not die; she just bowed out of my life. So did my father, and that is one wonderful thing you have...a kind and loving father." And the girls agreed that was true.

"We may not always agree on things," she added, "but I want you to be able to have your own opinions; you can express them and your feelings and believe *you* are *you*. You will not be an extension of me or anyone else. I will do everything in my power to help you grow into a kind and learned person who will help in every way you can to make the world a better place. It took a lot of faith and nerve for your father to leave you in my care. So we can do no less than our very best. I hope he will always be as proud of you as he is now."

* * * * *

One bright early spring morning, Jessica went along to school with her bag of peanut butter and crackers, an apple, and a little bag of chocolate cookies Mrs. Barrett had baked the evening before. Amanda watched her leave with a grateful heart that God had seen fit to send Jessica to her and her family. Her life was so pleasant and well organized she felt a sense of unease and a feeling that there was still a danger out there just waiting to happen and upset the even, moderate basis of her life.

Her home and family were too perfect and pleasing, and the feeling she had was that something else was going to happen, and it would not be something pleasant. She had been seeing John, and even though he had not been overly romantic, he had let her know he was attracted to her. She could not begin to understand why this wonderful, handsome man would spend time even looking at her. She saw with her own eyes that sometimes he did look at her with a glowing attention that could not be anything but attraction and something that was almost close to worship. If he could make her feel wanted and worthy, then why did he not find a way to tell her about what was going on in his mind and heart? She did not understand how a man's mind worked and could really say she did not understand her own heart. Some of the time, she wanted him to set something in motion to have her nearer to him when she sat in his car and in the movies. Then she felt a little prickle of tenseness and unease that made her scared of something, some kind of feeling that had a little bit of danger in it—an unrest. She was not afraid of John, yet there was a feeling of uncertainty in herself and an expectancy of the unknown.

Then, one morning, he called the store and asked her if she could come over to the office and visit awhile. Of course, she said she could and left the store with Thomas. When she walked into the Halsey Law Office, John and the judge were both there with their mugs of coffee, and her cup was on the coffee table. The very attitude in the office was too familiar. She again felt she was in a hole, trying to get up to level ground, but was slipping back each time she gained ground.

Then she said, "Oh Lord, what has happened now? What have I done wrong this time?"

"You have done nothing wrong," the judge said. "The other serpent has reared his ugly head. You know when the thing about Dermott happened, I told you there was at least one snake and a sidewinder we expected to give you a bad time. This is the sidewinder and should be the last of your troubles if we do what we need to do."

Then Amanda said, "Who?"

And John said, "Earnest Chalmers. We expected it months ago… We now hear from an attorney, out of Smith County, and he is asking for a settlement of ten thousand dollars damages for Earnest in the loss of his son and the grief he has gone through. He thinks the damages should be covered by your insurance, as the boy died on your property."

"But he didn't die on my property."

"We know that, but evidently Chalmers's lawyer doesn't. If he is any kind of respectable lawyer, he will look into the report in the sheriff's office and will back away from this case, or proceed with it in the hopes of an out of court settlement—hoping you will settle to avoid a lawsuit."

Amanda sat very still and tried to find some kind of opinion as to what had really happened the evening Boyd Chalmers had died on the sidewalk next to her driveway. If the questions arose as to why the boy had fallen backward and it meant Bubba would be brought into the case, she would try for a settlement out of court. Otherwise, she would meet any charges brought forth.

Then she turned to John and asked, "What do you think I should do?"

John, being John, as he had been so many times before, said, "Amanda, I think you know what you have to do. Regardless of feelings for others, the right way to do anything is the true and straightforward way, especially in a court of law."

Then she said, "Let's get on with it, then. If the court proves more people are involved in the outcome of Boyd's terrorizing me, then so be it. I am just glad I had someone to try to protect me." And she almost wept again—for Bubba, herself, and the Chalmers man who had reared a dangerous, unprincipled son.

"You are not the only one who is grateful for what happened to keep you safe. I have lost some sleep at night thinking about what could have happened." And John's face became suffused with red, the result of a mix of fear, anger, and thankfulness.

Then Amanda asked, "What are we to do to get ready for the trial? Are there witnesses to tell of Boyd and his exploits? There are none to speak about how and when it happened, as there was no one around when it happened. My neighbors said they heard nothing. Of course, Miles can tell about my tires being slashed, and maybe Howard might testify about the night that it all started and the fact Boyd promised to make me pay for getting away from them the night of the class stew and social. I think Howard felt terribly bad when he couldn't get them to take me home, but he couldn't fight Boyd and Marvin Jones both. Then, also, those girls could have dealt me misery, as they had been trying to pick a fight with me all the time I was with them. You can't imagine the awful things they said about me and what was going to happen to me." And she shivered again.

"We will offer to see Earnest in court and be surprised if the lawyer will be agreeable to put his reputation on the line. There is no real proof you contributed to the death of Boyd in any way."

That conversation kept coming back to Amanda as she put in her day in her business and when she and Jessie closed down the store for the night. She was not particularly afraid; she just felt down—not in a real depression—just tired of always having something hanging over her. It seemed every time she felt good or was making some progress with the store and the loans she was making to the people of the town, then something negative cropped up that took her mind off the wonderful people and Mr. C.'s dream.

The greatest pleasure she had, besides family, was John. He had gotten to the point he held her hand. They had gone to Greenville to the movies, had eaten together in the different restaurants there, and had gone together here in town to eat at Minningers, but he was careful not to be overly familiar or romantic in any sense. She had thought a time or two he was going to put his arms around her when he opened the car door for her; once or twice he almost did when he walked her to her door. But it didn't happen. And though she wondered how she could control the trembling his nearness caused, she still was anxious for him to touch her—to hold her.

She often wondered what he saw in her that made him want to spend time with her. Many times, in the still of the night in her bed, she let her imagination run away and could almost feel his kisses. She wanted them so badly she thought maybe she was sinning for thinking about them so much. She knew nothing of being sexually aroused, yet she felt there was something ahead for her that would change her whole outlook on life. Her body knew there was something she wanted.

Jessie had made all of them, Mrs. Barrett and Bubba and Amanda, so pleased with her good sense, wit, and enjoyment of living here with them that Amanda wondered how they had managed without her. The teacher, Miss Quaid, had been in the store a time or two and had told Amanda Jessica was a student who made teaching a pleasure. She said, "She is so thirsty for knowledge she makes the other teachers and me stay on our toes. She has even tutored some of the football and basketball boys so they can stay in sports." Then she picked up her sacks, and as usual, she left the store in a very businesslike manner.

Amanda got the sweetest, warmest feeling and wondered if Mr. C. could know about Jessie, and if he did, she felt he would be proud that she, Amanda, had learned from him to give something back after the blessing she had been given.

On that note she said her prayers and went to sleep without the depressing thought about the Chalmers man. She put away the picture in her mind of Earnest Chalmers for the night. But John stayed ever so close to her…The store and her time of study with Jessie kept the days moving along. Amanda found she still needed the Barretts, yet she loved the Sundays when she and Jessie puttered around the house after church, and for the first time, she learned how to cook a meal. Jessie was a good cook and was pleased they had a wonderful cookbook that had been Mrs. Leona's. Also, she was not afraid to experiment or substitute ingredients, so they waited expectantly to see and taste the results. At first, they thought they would be embarrassed to ask Mrs. Barrett to come for Sunday dinner after church, but they did, and she and Bubba seemed to enjoy their food.

The time the two girls spent with their study was very enjoyable. Working through the problems with two minds was better. Two minds would be quicker to solve a problem than one. Math had not been Amanda's favorite subject, yet having Jessica to work it down to plain and simple terms made it more fun and much easier.

Mrs. Smith, the librarian, asked them often to look at her lists of available books and help her decide which ones to order. The question was which ones would fit better with the folks in this part of Texas. Both girls were very conscientious to read about the books and wonder if the kids in school would be interested in them, and if the books would please the older readers.

Jessie was as pleasant to work with as anyone Amanda could imagine, as eager to learn anything about housework and the new appliances as she was the store business. She caught on to the washing machine with the rolling wringer and was as happy to change to the electric iron as she was the refrigerator with its ready-made ice. She went home some weekends, often enough to spend time with her dad, do some of his chores and cooking for him. Some of the time she rode her horse, Blinker, to town on Sunday evening, and that meant the Connor barn was in use again. It gave Bubba a great feeling, because he got to groom and feed a real live horse again. The horse stayed in the barn and the little patch by the garden until one of the days of the next week when Jessica's father came to the store for supplies and led him home behind the wagon…

Chapter 9

Amanda sat in the courtroom, waiting for the trial to start, and wondered if she would be called to testify. There were folks here from all over the county and some people she had never seen before. She felt most of them were here to see justice done, to see that this proceeding would be carried on in a fair and legal way. The judge was one she did not know, and she nervously looked down at John. He seemed pleased, so she decided not to worry about the judge and whether he would listen with an open mind.

She was glad the trial was finally happening. She had had this hanging over her for months now, taking time and energy from her business and Mr. C.'s plans for offering loans to depressed people. Then there were her studies with Jessica; she found it hard to concentrate while wondering and worrying about money. If she had to find enough to pay a greedy man whose unprincipled son had tried to wreck her life and abuse her body, then her help to the needy would taper off and maybe die a natural death.

The shadows of this day had left overcast skies on all her family, and, she felt, over the whole community. Most of the folks here today, she knew, were her friends, and she said a prayer this would end all, or at least almost all, of her trials and troubles. The only negative emotions she felt had happened when she had scanned the lawyers and had caught a glimpse of Earnest Chalmers at the table with his attorney. She had never in her life seen such hatred and diabolical wickedness as she saw on Earnest Chalmers's face. He had a smirky little grin on his face, as if he were enjoying himself.

The she looked back at John and saw enough optimism to again have some real hope, so she did not look at Chalmers and his lawyer again. When she had seen Chalmers, she had turned a little sick at her stomach and knew the man was anything but an upstanding citizen. He had not taught his son in any way to be an honorable, decent citizen, so…he had reaped what he had sowed. Deep in her heart, she felt if the judge ruled in Earnest Chalmer's favor, then there was no justice in this community or in the world. She would have to shut the doors to her business and stop going forward with Mr. C.'s plans to aid the citizens of the community. That would be a crying shame and a rank injustice.

Soon after the preliminaries, the person called to testify was Ben Miles. Chalmers's lawyer, Silas Brown, rose to his feet and asked Ben how long he had been the sheriff of the county. When Ben told him sixteen years, the lawyer seemed to falter a bit. Then he asked Ben where he was when he got the call to go to Mrs. Connor's home on the evening that Boyd Chalmers was found on Mrs. Connor's property.

At that point Ben said, "Mr. Brown, the body was not on the Connor property. There are pictures of the body and marks where the body was lying. If you have done your homework, you will not make erroneous statements such as that one." John could have called an objection to the lawyer's first real question, but as Ben had gone on record with a correction, he kept his seat. The lawyer was fairly civil as Ben recounted how the call had come to his home and the subsequent events, including Amanda's statement about what had happened to Boyd. The attorney questioned why no action had been taken to try to resuscitate the boy. Why no doctor had been called. Why no effort had been made to bring life back to his body. Ben was very precise and to the point of what had been done. He was reluctant but clear, saying that one look showed the back of the boy's head was crushed in, and there had been no pulse; the justice of the peace had come and recorded the death as accidental, and the case had been closed.

Then the attorney asked why Boyd was in the neighborhood to end up within inches of the Connor property. Ben said, "This was not the first time this young man had tried to follow Amanda Connor home. It seemed he had a vendetta of sorts against Mrs. Connor because she had gotten free of his car when he and some of his friends had refused to take her home, or to let her and her date leave the car after a class social."

Then the lawyer asked, "Was this so-called vendetta a known fact or was it only on the say-so of the Connor woman? Maybe a figment of her imagination?"

Ben looked the lawyer in the eye and said, "The people who are here today to see justice done are here to testify. A number of them are from the school, and two of them were in the car the night Boyd Chalmers swore to make Amanda Connor pay for getting away from him and his crowd. With the help of the boy she had a date with, they opened the back door of the automobile, and she willingly fell to the pavement from the moving car. She was lucky enough to hide from them to escape certain rape, degradation, and brutality, according to the threats made by the deceased, as heard by the witnesses. That was what he swore to do to her. The crowd was drinking 'white lightnin' whiskey' from Sugar Hill. White lightning is a distilled whiskey, homemade by some folks who live in the north end of Canes County. By the way, all the students I talked to said this was the first date the then sixteen-year-old Amanda Connor had ever had."

The attorney stopped to look at his notes and then asked, "Why was the girl in a car with people she did not know?"

Then Ben said, "It is my understanding this was the first month Mrs. Connor had transferred from a common school district to Canesville High School, and the first class social she had been invited to attend. I think the boy who invited her is here and will testify as to how it happened that he and Mrs. Connor were riding in the Chalmers car."

"Then tell us more about the so-called vendetta, Mr. Miles."

And Ben Miles said, "Back last fall, she had escaped from him in her car once, before the night of his death, by rocking her automobile back and forth to break his hold on her upper arm. I saw the bruises on the defendant the night that happened. When she called me to report the incident, she asked I go by her parking lot to see if Boyd Chalmers was out there and needed help.

"Then, the night he died, he was chasing her on foot, as he had slashed both right tires on her automobile to keep her from getting away from him."

The attorney looked shocked. He stopped to whisper to Earnest Chalmers for a few minutes. Then he cleared his throat before asking the judge for a recess. After some consultation between Earnest and his lawyer, the judge asked both attorneys to approach the bench.

Silas Brown and John Halsey went to the judge's desk, and the judge said, "Mr. Brown, what are you trying to prove? You are asking for several thousand dollars damage from Mrs. Connor for Mr. Chalmers, just because his son fell down *just short* of Mrs. Connor's property and cracked his skull. Tell us just how you intend to prove she did an injustice to him or his father. Do you believe the lady, who is possibly five feet, three inches tall, threw him down and broke his head? Now, we are sorry Mr. Chalmers's son died, but it would be past believability to say Mrs. Connor is responsible for his death, since he was chasing her trying to keep her from entering her home. She was not touching him when he fell, so the sheriff's records show, and I don't believe there is or ever will be a case against her. There have been no criminal charges brought against her, and no one seems to believe she did anything wrong by trying to defend herself by getting away from his clutches."

At that time Earnest Chalmers started yelling, "That's a lie." Over and over he yelled, "It's a lie. It's a lie."

Then the lawyer asked the judge if he could spend more time with his client and went back to the table to try to talk to the man who was so angry and wild he was screaming and fuming.

The courtroom was quiet except for the awful noises Earnest Chalmers was making. It was a fact the two men were arguing, and the attorney was stuffing papers into his attaché case and shaking his head. It was very apparent the lawyer was through with his part of the whole thing. The other man was furious and was mouthing curses and filthy language.

The judge pounded his gavel and said, "Both attorneys approach the bench. And I instruct Mr. Chalmers to be quiet." The man did not get quiet. He became louder and louder and began to spew curses, hate, and threats in a loud and screeching voice.

The judge pounded his gavel again and again and finally said, "Bailiff, take the man in custody, even if you have to handcuff him. He is in contempt of this court."

The people in the courtroom were still quiet, except for Chalmers, and the only person who offered to help the bailiff put the cuffs on Chalmers was Jimmy Barnes, and he seemed to be enjoying having a knee in the vile man's back.

Then the judge stood and declared he was throwing the case out of court, and he swept from the courtroom. The gesture was the same as she had read about in so many books, and she felt a sense of having been a real part of a startling but somber drama.

Amanda heaved a sigh of relief and noticed the people were forming a quiet, unhurried line and were coming to her. The hugs, handshakes, and best wishes took quite some time. When the room was almost empty, Amanda began trying to find a way to say more than "thank you" to these people and the Lord for the support she had that afternoon. It took a while for everyone to pass by, and she did not tire of their care and concern.

When she turned toward the door, she noticed two more people coming very slowly toward the front of the room. She turned completely around to watch her mother and father make some progress down the aisle.

She stood very still to see if they would come all the way. When they got close enough that she could see tears in her mother's eyes, she moved into the aisle and opened her arms to clasp them both.

Her dad coughed, and she knew that was because of the old beliefs that "grown men don't cry."

The three of them stood still, and not one of them was in a hurry to say anything or to ask anything of each other.

Amanda wanted to say "Thank you, Lord" aloud, but she did not.

Her mother wanted to say "Forgive me," but she could not.

Her father wanted to say "Finally," and he tried to say it, but he had no breath, and his vocal chords were paralyzed.

Just then John came through the back door with his insouciant grin on his face and said, "Hey, folks, let's get out of here. I just left Mrs. Barrett and Bubba at the house, and she said the chicken is ready to fry. Until you eat her fried chicken, you've not had fried chicken."

Amanda's heart was full when she guided the others out to the big automobile. She looked first at her mother and then her father. She looked at John, who had done so much to get her through these trying times, and then she looked up and said, "How have we done, Mr. C.?"

John quietly said, "You did just fine, Mrs. C.!"

Amanda's parents stopped beside the car and were prepared to say goodbye before making their way home. Amanda dragged some air into her lungs. "Maybe you could stay for the meal? Mrs. Barrett usually cooks plenty, especially when we are headed for the weekend, because we all like leftovers."

John said, "And her leftovers are to die for."

Evelyn Mason looked at Amanda and said, "Amanda, we didn't come to the hearing wanting something from you. We just wanted you to know you were on our hearts and in our prayers."

"No, Mama, that was not the reason you came. You came because I asked God to bring you here. I have tried to do the things

Mr. C. and the Lord wanted me to do, but…being a failure with my family was my deepest sorrow."

"But you never have been a failure. The failure was our own doing," said her father as he turned away to hide his tears and his plea for forgiveness.

Then Amanda's mother said, "Amanda, you were what brought us together in the first place. Then you were what pulled us apart, but you were what kept us together in the years past when maybe we should not have been together. We failed you because we never settled our differences and worked to make a home with some love and caring. Our 'together' was not enough for us to love you and show it. We finally understand why we were so suspicious of you through your time with us. We could not trust ourselves, so we could not trust others, even you."

"I know, Mama. Mr. C. told me there must have been mistrust of yourselves in your lives. It doesn't matter now."

John was listening attentively, but now he said, "OK, folks, let's go to Amanda's house and celebrate with the fried chicken. Remember that I had a first today. I won a case in court without having to call one witness for the sued. I won the case without getting hard-boiled with a man who is the most venomous, spiteful person I have met. I am sorry, in a way, the trial didn't continue for a little while. I think it could have made some lasting impressions on some of our schoolkids…a bigger impression than I did last Sunday in Sunday school."

Amanda said, "John, you didn't."

And he said, "It was a ready-made occasion for it."

And Amanda's mother said, "It was for me too."

Amanda helped her mother into the back seat of the car, with her father hesitantly getting in through the other back door. Then she sat with John as he drove them to her house. Her heart was full, and John reached over, picked up her hand, and held it close against his thigh. He had never done that before; she looked up at him, and he turned his head enough to give her a quiet, restrained smile. It seemed special at the time, and she got that funny little feeling something was going on in her body as well as her mind.

Mrs. Barrett did not seem surprised Amanda's parents were there, and as John said, the meal was superb and was thoroughly enjoyed. They all sat around the long table, and Amanda felt John enjoyed her parents, Mrs. Barrett, Bubba, Jessica, and Amanda.

When the meal was over and the finer points of the day in court had been discussed, John told them the other lawyer had talked to him on the phone. He said he had realized the man was a very respectable attorney, and he had relaxed after their conversation. He did not want the lawyer to quit beforehand, as he thought Earnest might have come up with a high-powered shyster. Also, he did not want to discuss the charges with the attorney, because he had been afraid they might think John would try for an out-of-court settlement. "In fact," he said, "I am still a little disappointed Judge Williams threw it out so soon. I still thought some of the young people should have seen how easy it is to get into trouble with the wrong crowd. That was one of the reasons the two Civics (Government) classes and one History class were brought to hear the trial."

And then Amanda said, "I wondered why so many young people were there. Was Jessica there?"

John laughed and said, "She told me beforehand she would be there, but she didn't want you to see her—and you didn't. Right?" She shook her head, for she had not seen Jessica.

When everyone was leaving the table, Evelyn Mason and Mrs. Barrett picked up dishes from the table and started stacking them by the sink in the kitchen. Jessica appeared like magic and filled the dishpan with hot, soapy water. She was introduced to Amanda's mother. Mrs. Barrett and Evelyn moved to the living room. John and her father had moved to the front porch and seemed to be getting along fine. It was pretty cold out, but Amanda thought her dad was having a smoke and, for that, would brave anything.

She wandered about the house and felt a little giddy with no threats hanging over her for the first time in months. Part of her restlessness was the way she felt about John. How in the world could she even think an educated, professional man would look at a high school dropout still in her teens? It made no sense at all, but she knew he did look at her sometimes as though he enjoyed seeing her. He seemed to love watching her and some of the things she did and said.

Something else she noticed often: he never refuted her opinions as she stated them. The only time he seemed to have a question, he asked her if maybe she could take a little more time with her decisions. When she agreed, he usually posed two different ways of looking at an issue and gave her a choice. Otherwise, he seemed to accept her as she was, just as C. H. Connor had.

As her dad and John came into the living room, John asked if the Masons were ready to go home. Then his eyes wandered the room until he found Amanda, and he asked if she would ride with him to her dad's house so she could drop him off at the courthouse for his car on the way back.

The ride to her old home was quiet, yet it was not unpleasant. John asked her dad if the roads on out were still as bad as they used to be, and her dad said, "Yes, some of the time, when it rains, they are impassable for cars and trucks."

When the ride was over and her parents were getting out, they both were saying good night as they made their way to the house, and Amanda and John said good night too. When they were gone, Amanda drew a soft but long breath and sat lower in her seat.

John said, "Amanda, you handled that with your folks like a pro. You have had to grow up way too fast, but you are the most mature person for your age I have ever known. You have carried on a business and Mr. C.'s plans just as any mature and experienced person could have. You haven't buckled under problems, and you've never whined. I think it is now time for you to find another kind of love. Have you felt a little, tiny jolt of it?"

She said, "I don't know. What am I looking for?"

John said, "You'll know when you feel it. Right?"

The ride out had seemed long, but the ride back to town was much too short. They were back at the stately building that was the courthouse in no time at all—not enough time at all for her to reply to John's question.

Amanda turned in her seat to seek out more about what he had asked and to tell him how much she appreciated his day in court and taking her parents home. When she turned to him, his face was right there, and they almost bumped noses. Then she said, "Oh, I am sorry," and she tried to pull away, to move back a space. John followed her and put his arms around her, so there was no place for retreat.

He chuckled and said, "Quit trying to run away from me. I have let you do that way too long to suit me, but no more."

"What do you mean? I've never run away from *you*! I thought, at times, you were going to move in close; you seemed to think about it, and then *you* moved away." Then, of all the things she could have done or said, she giggled.

John chuckled and said, "Amanda, be quiet and hold still. If this is your first kiss, and I believe it is, then let's get it right."

He looked into her eyes and gently lowered his face to hers, and his lips fit on hers. She closed her eyes and held her breath, and everything flew out of her mind. And...she felt robbed when his lips left hers. He raised his head up and back to look at her. Then her big, dark-rimmed eyes opened, and she thought she would never breathe again.

"Oh, my," she said.

Then John asked, "Well, how was it?"

Amanda said, "It...it was...very nice."

"Nice? Is that the best I can do? Just nice?"

She said, "Well...maybe we could practice more. We are going to try it again before you leave?"

"Yes, Amanda, we are going to try it again. But we better start planning a wedding really soon, because kissing you will never be enough. I want you in my heart, in my mind, and in my bed as soon as possible. Will you marry me, Amanda?"

"Well...let's try the kiss again, and if it is *nice* again, I think the answer is *yes*. OK?"

He held her as close as was comfortable to them, and the kiss started out nice and...sweet. It then became questing, searching, and heated. Very heated. When she opened her eyes, he searched them for an answer and said, "Nice? Yes?"

And she said, "*Ooh la la! Yes, yes, yes!*"

*****

As Amanda worked, it was on her mind constantly how very lucky she was to have such wonderful people who had helped and guided her through her fast-growing-up time. There had been John, his dad Hap, and Ben Miles. There had been Mrs. Barrett, who had done so much to save Amanda's energy for her work in her business and on Mr. C's project. And there was Bubba, that wonderful child who had protected her and possibly saved her life. If not her life, he had saved her from untold pain and degradation.

He had never mentioned the part he had played in the awful debacle when Boyd Chalmers had died. Maybe Bubba had shut it out of his mind, and she hoped that he had, because he had a very tender heart even about animals. She sensed he did not think he had done any wrong, or he would have fretted. If he had felt he had hurt someone or done anything bad, his actions would have let somebody know. He certainly would have been hyper and fretful.

She searched her own heart and mind about her part in all that had happened, and she honestly believed it could not have ended safely in any other way. She actually felt free of guilt, as she had felt she had not had a choice. She had been on a rocky ride with no way to get off. As long as Boyd Chalmers had lived and been allowed to run rampant over the people he came in contact with, especially the young people, things would have gotten worse.

After the trial, she had been nervous about Earnest Chalmers and wondered if he would take up the vendetta Boyd had started. Then she was told he was under a peace bond, had gone through a contempt of court proceeding, and had been made to feel the safest thing for him to do was leave Northeast Texas. He, evidently, had been transferred in his job of measuring land under cultivation for the government to another part of the state.

Now she wondered when John would decide they should plan their wedding and was anxious to be with him as much as possible. She worried and fretted about her lack of education and ignorance of what mature men and women did to build a home and life together. If their kisses were the forerunner of what happened between a man and his wife, she felt inept and uncertain about her ability to bring pleasure to such a mature and experienced man. She wondered what in the world he saw in her when there were so many beautiful girls and women around. She was very sure she would be an embarrassment to him. She had seen Miss Lloyd, the third-grade teacher, look at her almost with scorn when John had looked at her and smiled as they waited in line to buy tickets for the movie. It had shaken her, so she had not smiled back. This had caused him to slide his eyes sideways to the face of Samantha Lloyd, and then he had grinned outright. He was almost determined to see she knew he was glad to be with her, and he wanted everybody to know it.

Chapter 10

Now what was on her mind was the fact John had asked her to marry him. She had told him she would, but she still thought he could do a lot better than a pitiful little girl from the country that sorely needed an education. She knew she was going to marry him, and she still did not know why, when they were together, he seemed anxious to kiss and hold her, but not for long at a time.

They had started going places together, really dating, and he wanted her to sit close to him, yet some of the time, he seemed terribly nervous. When he was nervous, she always sensed it, for he sang, whistled, and tapped on the steering wheel or a desk or a table, whatever was available.

When they said good night, she loved it, for she felt free to raise her arms and put them around his neck. Once she put her fingers into his hair at the back of his neck, and he went still, very still. Then he took her arms down and mumbled, "That is enough."

Then she said, "Oh, John, did I do something wrong?"

And he said, "No, Amanda, you do everything just right. Can you set the date for our wedding? Can you make it soon, very soon?"

"John, am I supposed to do that? I kept waiting for you to tell me when, and when you didn't, I thought you were in no hurry." She was troubled and was chewing on her lip.

He said, "Lord, Amanda, if I had thought it was my place to set the date, I would have had it the next day after you said, 'yes'!"

"Then we will do it Saturday. Will that be soon enough?" she asked.

So the next day, she went to Mrs. Albany's shop and asked her if she had a dress that would do for her to wear next Saturday to her wedding.

Mrs. Albany said, "Maybe. But wouldn't you like to go over to Dallas and find a real wedding dress? One that has been made especially for a bride? After all, you are only going to do this one more time, and just think how much fun we could have shopping for the very perfect and just right dress."

Amanda thought and chewed her lip for a bit, then said, "Let me see what you have. I have a million things to do to have the store ready for Thomas, Jessie, and one part-time help to keep it going until I get back. Oh, and do you have a fairly nice dress that Jessie can wear? I haven't asked her yet, but I want her to be my bridesmaid."

Mrs. Albany said, "Amanda, I have a darling off-white two-piece dress in the sheerest, softest wool you will ever hope to see. When it came in, I immediately saw it on you. You must have it even if you don't wear it for the wedding."

She went to the back and brought it out. Amanda could see it was what Mrs. Albany had said. The material was so soft that when you gathered some of it in your hand, it looked fluffy. Amanda took it to the fitting room and put it on. She was as amazed as she had been when she had tried on the deep green dress Mr. C. had bought for her. She loved the dress. She loved the way it made her feel.

"Mrs. Albany, I don't know how you know just exactly what is just right for me, but I love this dress. I will need a couple more, not so dressy, to take with me. While you are looking for them, I will see what I can find over here for Jessie. I think the dress we bought here for her was what? A size seven?"

"Where are you going on the honeymoon? I know it's none of my business, but it would help us pick out the right clothes."

Amanda laughed and said, "John said it was none of my business either. That I would love it because he intended to make me so happy and in love, the whole world would look like a rainbow." And both of them giggled.

"Well, you have done something to that man nobody else has ever been able to do. He has turned into a romantic, almost overnight."

Then Amanda said, "John says even he can't believe it. He doesn't say he is a romantic; he says he is worse than a teenager with nothing in his body except hormones." And both of them laughed again.

Amanda was well pleased with her purchases, and when she and Jessie got home and ate their supper, she said, "Jessie, I want you to do something for me..."

And Jessie said, "Amanda, you know I will do anything for you. Gladly."

"I know you want to, but we have to agree you will be at ease with this. I know your dad is coming to stay part of the time next week while we are gone, and I think is lovely for you two to be together. But you know we are going to marry here. I think my dad will, supposedly," and she grinned, "give me away, and the judge will stand with John, but I don't have anyone to be with me. I don't have a sister or a best friend to be with me. Would you consider being my bridesmaid? I think of you as both my best friend and my little sister."

She watched Jessie closely as the girl took in what she was saying, and then Jessie's face turned red before turning pasty white so the little freckles across her nose stood out.

Then Jessie said, "Oh, I just couldn't. I don't know how to act, and I don't have anything to wear, and…and…"

And Amanda took her in her arms and said, "That's what all little sisters say, especially the first time. Don't you remember the one in "Love Is Not a Game"? Can you do it for me?"

Jessica felt that she *was* Amanda's little sister. There was not much difference in their ages, but Amanda was light years ahead of her in her business life and real maturity. She did not know Amanda felt the same way about herself. She felt she was not ready to be a wife of such a wonderful man. Deep down she was panic-stricken she would be a failure as his wife in this, another new life. To fail would be fatal, because she loved John Halsey so much she did not think she could live if she disappointed him. And she told Jessica all her doubts and fears and how much she needed her to stand up and hold her bouquet for her while she helped with John's ring and her own. Amanda knew she needed Jessica to steady her to keep her from falling on her face. Jessica said she would. The girls laughed for hours at the word pictures they made up for the mythical wedding they talked into existence.

It seemed John was in the store and her home constantly. Wherever she was, at any given time, he appeared to materialize, and she became accustomed to looking up and finding his ready smile turned her way. She became so addicted to his presence that if he was tied up in court or was doing office work she felt disappointed. He reminded her constantly that Saturday was too far away. He told her he had his best suit ready, and the license, and felt they should just have his dad say the words and go along on their honeymoon.

Then Saturday morning came, and Amanda checked and re-checked luggage to make sure she had packed all the things she could need for the week she would be gone. She had taken a little time out on Friday to go over to talk to Dr. Story. She asked him if she needed to do anything about birth control, and if there was any-thing she needed to do to have her body prepared for her wedding night. She was very embarrassed to speak of this to anyone, but she trusted Doctor Story and hoped he did not think her too forward.

He said, "Amanda, you are a very smart girl to be concerned about things, but I know John is a very caring person. I am sure he will see you are cared for, and he will be prepared to take precau-tions in the use of contraceptives. You have come a long way since the first time you came to see me." And he put his arm around her shoulders and squeezed.

"But," he continued, "you have had to grow up fast and face a lot of decisions. It must be time for life to be kind to you, and you are not going to need anything besides the love that shines in John Halsey's eyes." Then he handed her a little package and watched her walk down the street, just as he had the first time she had come to see him.

Amanda dropped the little package in her purse and did not see it again until she was down on the coast with her husband and needed it. She was very grateful to the kindly doctor who let her have what she needed without embarrassing her. It was a tube of K-Y Jelly.

The wedding was a success to all who were involved. John had thought Amanda was the most beautiful he had seen her. He thought the only time she might be more so would be when, and if, she was carrying his baby. He wanted her to be a little older for that. She was due a little time of fun, peace, and unqualified love. She had a lot of love coming to her from many people and from many directions, but she had worked hard to earn all that love and devotion. Now it was time to lay aside her awesome tasks of being there for her family and extended family and simply live and be cared for.

When he stood in her living room, waiting for her to walk in from the stairway, John couldn't stop moving forward and back from his heels to the balls of his feet. Then his dad placed his hand on John's forearm and said in a quiet voice, "Simmer down, son, you have been patient, waiting all these years, so twenty minutes is a snap!"

John turned and hugged his dad and said, "I know, I know. But this is the only girl in the world I have loved, and I can't wait until she is mine."

Jessie left the stairway, a pretty picture in the robin's-egg blue dress, carrying a small bouquet of yellow roses Bubba had picked and Amanda had helped him put together in a bouquet. Then Amanda and her dad came down the steps, and she took everybody's breath away. The soft two-piece dress was so "just right for her" and was the epitome of innocence and purity, but it still showed her body in a very beautiful, sensual way, and she almost seemed to glow. John was absolutely stunned, and everyone could see it.

Amanda's father stopped on the bottom step of the stairs and looked at Amanda with tears very openly filling his eyes and said, "Amanda, I would give my life if it would wipe out the awful things

I did and said to you. You are the finest lady I have ever known, and I can't believe you gave me this honor. You know I don't deserve it." Then he braced his shoulders and proudly escorted her across the room to the little altar arch that was set up in front of the fireplace. There he placed her hand in John's and said, "Bless you both." And his gait was stiff and jerky as he passed back to sit beside Evelyn Mason.

John took her hand, turned toward the minister, and hoped he would find his voice when the time came to say "I do!"

Amanda turned to hand her bouquet of deep red roses to Jessie. She raised her wonderful, expressive face to John, and what he saw was her deep, dark eyes and the promise there.

They exchanged the rings they had bought in Greenville from Mr. C.'s friend, and John lost his thinking powers and his voice. Judge Hap pushed her ring into John's hand, a gentle reminder the wedding must go on. The vows were pledged, and then everybody was talking at once. They waited to be congratulated, and then the two of them slipped upstairs to change for their trip.

When John came from Mr. C.'s room to the door of Amanda's bedroom, he said, "Do you really want to go back down there?"

And she said, "Not particularly." As soon as they stopped to enjoy the kiss both were so anxious for, John held the window in the back of the bedroom up, and she stepped out onto the roof of what used to be a washhouse. They jumped down to the ground, raced to John's car, and were gone with some cans and one cowbell clanging along behind them up the street and around the square. A lot of wonderful folks came to attention to find out what the noise was all about, and they waved and called, "Good luck."

Then John said, "OK, Mrs. Halsey, wave to your subjects!" And she did.

The love they had pledged to each other meant more to them than the right to make love to each other. That part was soon happily accomplished and was almost sacred to them. They promised each other a lifetime of love, beauty, and worship of each other's hearts, minds, and bodies.

For the first time in her life, Amanda went to a dine-and-dance club. When John had mentioned it, she was flabbergasted. "But I can't dance. I don't know how. My church didn't believe in dancing, and besides, I didn't have anyone to teach me."

"Well, now you do have somebody to teach you. All you have to do is hum, and I'll show you the old box step. It's a snap. When you master that, you can dance to anything that has any rhythm or tune. You see, my old alma mater is having our class reunion, and it is a must that we go. It is a must we dance; it is a must I hold you close to my pounding heart." And she did learn how to dance.

When Amanda saw the Gulf of Mexico, all the things she had read about Texas, the states of the Union, and the oceans of the world became meaningful to her. She loved the sand and found John loved it also and pulled his shoes off and played in the sugary substance with her. He supported her wish to act as a child, and for the first time in her life, she allowed herself to play and act like a young girl. It was a heavenly time for her, and John gloried in her joy. He gloried in her seeing and doing some of the things she had only dreamed of in her stringent, sparsely peopled existence.

They took long walks and ate in some of the best cafes. One of the best meals they enjoyed was wieners roasted over a tiny fire built of driftwood, half-burnt marshmallows, and Cokes from little twelve-ounce green bottles. Amanda's eyes were so expressive that John enjoyed her pleasure and excitement time and again. The weather was great, as was the pleasure they found in seeing and doing the things they found out of the ordinary for Northeast Texans.

They loved each other's stories of their youth and childhood and became accustomed to sharing their minds, hearts, and bodies. It was a wonderful week. Even though Amanda was anxious to return to her extended family, friends, and business, she felt a loss when the time came for this idyll to end.

Then the bride and groom, on the last day of their honeymoon, were full of plans for their future as they drove into town from the south, rounded the square, and turned down the street to her house. She said, "John, can you imagine what Mr. C. would say today if he could talk to us?"

"Yes, Amanda, I know what he would say, because he talked about it in my office soon after you were married."

"You are kidding. Right?"

"No, Amanda." John studied her for a second, and then he said, "He told me his only concern about what he had done for you was that your in-name-only marriage might interfere with your ability to find real love. His term of real love and marriage, I thought, meant you could have a traditional marriage and rear a family."

"Well, I can tell the world I have that kind of marriage and love… And to think my first taste of love of any kind was from him and to him. Had he not been so caring and kind, I may have gone through my life not ever knowing what life is for and how to accept it."

They drove into the garage, and Amanda stepped out of the car, and her knees knocked. This was a different homecoming. It was the start of a whole new life, just as that other homecoming to this house had been.

The lights were on in the kitchen, but she could see no one. Inside she found the table set beautifully, even with candles ready to light. John sniffed around until he found the fried chicken in the warmer oven, and Amanda dished up the vegetables and poured the iced tea. This was their first real meal together, for in the cafes where they had eaten, he could not hold her hand and play footsy under the table. He had not felt free to tell her just how beautiful she was and how he was going to make love to her. When he had tried to do those things in public, she had become very red-faced and could not eat much. He had realized they were, to anyone looking at them, a picture of young lovers. To his chagrin, he then had to become businesslike and change the subject to something mundane and uninteresting.

Tonight the ambiance was just what was needed for them to declare again how much they loved each other and how happy they were.

When the meal was over, they did the few dishes and strolled upstairs. She was sure everything was perfect in the room she had slept in alone during the time she had lived in this house. The bed was even turned down, and yet she was not ready to retire, so she said, "Do you want to see my communing place?"

John said, "Of course, I want to see and know everything about you." She picked up a quilt and two pillows and put them through the window to the porch outside, to the gallery that was really the roof of the lower porch. When she crawled through, John was right behind her.

So she spread the quilt and lay down. She put her head on one pillow, laid the other by hers, and motioned for him to crawl on the quilt beside her. She put his face between her hands and said,

"I love you, John Halsey, and I hope we live here together at least fifty years."

He looked into her dark-ringed eyes and said, "I love you, Amanda Halsey, and I hope we live together like this at least a hundred centuries." The two of them lay quietly with their hands touching faces. Amanda felt love roll over them and bathe them in a soft pink glow as she looked up into the heavens. She felt acceptance coming from all around, and knew, deep in her heart, Mr. C. and Mrs. Leona were smiling at her, her husband, and *their* house.

"If we are going to sleep out here, we have to have more cover," John commented as he moved to hold her close and rub his raspy chin over her smoother cheek.

She said, "Don't whine. We are not going to sleep out here until warm weather, but I wanted you to know about my place I have found to commune with God...and with Mr. C."

"Then, if we are going to use it as a deck, maybe I should re-floor it and put some doors from the bedrooms to this...our communing place."

And then he stretched and yawned, and she said, "Maybe you should put rails around it so that little Connor Halsey doesn't fall off it." She threw her arms around his neck and said, "You would like to name our first son for Mr. C.?"

"But Connor?" he rumbled. "Well, that was your last name until last Saturday." And he grinned.

"Yes, it might as well have been my maiden name, because I was prouder of that than I was of Mason. And the alternative to Connor is not great." She seemed a little puzzled.

He looked at her and asked, "That is?"

"Herbert. Could you picture naming our firstborn Herbert?"

"Not on your life. I have known some nice fellows named Herbert. And then there is the unpopular ex-president, and most of the other Herberts became Herb. How did you find out?"

Then she giggled and said, "He wasn't happy about it, but the man at the jewelry store in Greenville called him Herbert. It seemed they had gone to college together." And she added, "He looked so embarrassed I never teased him about it. Especially about our famous, or infamous, president of that name."

"That's my loving and generous wife. Wife, crawl through that window. We are going to have to find you a warmer place to build air castles in. Right?"

"Right." And she made a beeline to the right side of the bed, because they had, supposedly, already settled that argument of which of them slept where in the bed. Still she wasn't sure he wouldn't poach on her side just to have a reason to tickle and tussle her.

Then Amanda thought back to all the things that had happened to her in the last two years, and she looked up and wondered if she was good enough and smart enough to be worthy of all her blessings. Still, she felt like the scared and ignorant little girl she had been when Mr. C. saw her and offered her a job was just a day or two back from where she was at this moment.

The wonderful man who was at this time showering and shaving just so she could sleep next to him and enjoy every minute of the night she adored. This wonderful man was a blessing she could not compare to anything else in the world.

So, when he was finished, she looked up into his loving face and said, "I love you, John, so much I can't begin to tell you how much."

And he said, "You don't have to say it often, only once or twice each hour, because those eyes, with the turquoise rings, are very expressive and say it a lot. I hope they never quit saying it. The first time I came here to help you find the box, those eyes made me know they were a part of something I wanted. That wanting grew until I was almost dying all the time I wasn't with you. I almost quit work, so Dad said, and mooned around like a teenager."

"Well, I was and am a teenager, and the few times I thought you were attracted to me scared me to death. Even after I knew you wanted me, I could not believe you would want me for forever, and I could not see myself refusing you anything. I only knew I would try and refuse if I was strong enough."

John said, "Amanda, I would never have asked that of you. You are too fine, good, and upstanding. At the time, when Boyd Chalmers was harassing you, I wanted to do away with him. I think Miles knew, and it caused him to try hard to handle it. I think that was one thing that caused him to talk to the boy and Earnest. He himself began to doubt he could handle Boyd and his evil little game in an equitable and morally right manner."

Amanda said, "Yes, he told me. This is the last time we are going to talk about those awful times. I thank the Lord, Mr. C., Miles, your dad, and this whole community for helping me become a businessperson and find love and self-respect. But most of all, I thank you. "You treated me as an adult when others were pulling me down, just as Carter did when he said, 'Just stay over there and run your little store while we men take care of the banking business.'"

John sat on the left side of the bed, gathered her up into his arms, and said, "You are perfect, Mrs. Halsey, and are worth all the misery I went through waiting to make my case with you."

She giggled, "Now I know when you were suffering."

"You don't have any idea."

But she said, "You whistled, hummed, and tapped on your desk or the steering wheel." She ran to the bathroom and tried to close the door. Then he tickled her, and she giggled. She realized she laughed a lot now and thanked Mr. C. because he had taught her how to laugh with his wry humor, off-the-wall sayings, and silly little songs. Plus the big fat lies he mouthed about the sardines and other things, just to see her crack up. She remembered when he had sung his little ditties with their inane verses just to teach her how to laugh, to become acquainted with happiness, to find love and some fun in her existence. He had told her that to hear her really laughing and almost carefree was one of his greatest pleasures.

Later, with her head on John's shoulder, she prayed the little prayer she always had. Amanda realized it had changed some, as when she had prayed it as a child. She had been asking for help and things she needed and felt the Lord *could* answer but probably wouldn't. Her faith had been weak, and she had felt she did not deserve much. She knew she was not good enough to warrant the Lord's interest. When she had told Mr. C. she was not worthy of all the blessings that had come to her, he had said, "How do you know I am worthy of all the blessings that have been mine?"

Deep down in her heart she felt her wonderful Mr. C. deserved, if anyone she had ever known did, blessings. Anyway, most of her prayers were "thank-yous" now.

Chapter 11

When Sunday morning came, Amanda and John were eager to do their bit of housekeeping and breakfast in their lovely kitchen. Amanda was proud she could manage a meal of biscuits, scrambled eggs, and bacon. Jessica had taught her those things and to be very careful to measure the water, the coffee, and the minutes the pot perked so she knew the coffee was just right. When John tasted it he said, "Um, Mrs. Halsey, this coffee is divine. Much better than I make, and I have an electric coffee maker. Maybe you can teach me how, now that I live here."

And Amanda said, "If you bring that newfangled coffee maker here, I bet Mrs. Barrett will stash it back somewhere, and it'll never see daylight again."

"Well, it can't improve on this or Mrs. Barrett's coffee." Then he lowered his voice as though that redoubtable lady might hear him and said, "I do believe this coffee is tastier than hers. But...that will be our secret. Right?"

And Amanda said, "It better be. I learned a long time ago one is never to do anything to usurp her rule in this kitchen."

When the kitchen was tidy, Amanda and John dressed and walked the three blocks over to the little brick church Mr. C. had loved and supported. Everyone was friendly and pleased Amanda was back in town and in the church.

Amanda felt this was one of her last tests. If the people here in this church body accepted her as a married woman, married to an upstanding attorney they all knew, than maybe her life was on the way to being a success. She had a full slate of things to do in the future: She would run her business, hire more help, and take the college entrance exam. She would start classes and would continue to make some loans to folks who needed them.

Then she looked up instead of bowing her head and asked silently, "Dear Lord, look over us all, and may our mistakes be few and small?"

There was a war going on in Europe, and that dark cloud was drawing closer and turning darker and denser. She prayed for the leaders of the world, her country, and this, her community.

*****

Life became a wonderful series of events for Amanda, and she knew her whole family was happy and almost contented. The economy was beginning a slow recovery, and farm prices were better than they had been in many years. There were more jobs outside of the agriculture community. People began some building projects in addition to the Works Progress Administration (WPA), a government-subsidized program that was building schools, libraries, and local government buildings. The long drought was easing some, and the outlook was positive for a change.

Jessica finished high school in the upper 10 percent of the big graduation class of 1939. The class was big because few jobs had been available to the teenagers, so they went to high school to pass the time until they could find employment. Everyone seemed to find some money somewhere to do what had to be done. Amanda commuted to Commerce to attend East Texas State Teachers College on "A" days: Mondays, Wednesdays, and Fridays during the fall and spring terms.

Then pain and sadness struck again.

One spring morning, Mrs. Barrett was late coming to the house to fix breakfast for John, Amanda, and Jessica. John usually ate with the two girls after they were dressed and ready to leave the house for classes in Commerce. When Mrs. Barrett arrived, Amanda and Jessie already had the bacon and the eggs whipped up and ready to scramble. They turned to look as she came through the door and saw the pain and sadness on her face.

The John asked, "What happened, Mrs. B.?"

And she said, "Bubba is sick, and Dr. Story thinks it is his appendix. Would you go over and help load him into the car to take him to the hospital?" And of course, John wiped his mouth and rushed to do what he could to help.

Amanda went to Mrs. Barrett and said, "Oh Lord, Mrs. Barrett, is he bad? I know he has been draggy the last couple of days, but they'll take out the appendix and he'll be fine. Won't he?"

Then Mary Barrett said, "I don't know. Dr. Story said we should have told him sooner, but Bubba pretended he was all right. He was frightened, you know, of shots, the doctor, and mostly the hospital, because he said people who went to the hospital died. He hates shots so much he pretended he was fine, and I only saw at three o'clock this morning he was bad. When the doctor came, Bubba was in such pain and misery he was having convulsions. Dr. Story says his appendix has ruptured, and we'll probably lose him." The last sentence was a keening wail.

Amanda was hard put to hold Mrs. Barrett, and she felt she could not argue with the mother of the twenty-year-old boy who was, for all practical purposes, a six-year-old child. She waited for John to come home and tell her Bubba was in the hospital, Dr. Story was scrubbed, and he and young Dr. Pitt were ready to operate.

Then she asked if she should go to the hospital with Mrs. Barrett, and that lady looked her in the face and said, "Please?" So she did. The hours dragged by as they waited for the surgery to be completed, and Amanda wondered how her wonderful Mrs. B. could be halfway calm and accepting of what she feared—they both feared—would be the outcome of this day.

Then Mrs. Barrett said, "You know Dr. Story told me when Bubba was born he probably would not live to be grown. He said the lifespan of the severely retarded was never very long, but Bubba was not severely retarded. Mr. C. H. was able to teach him to work and grow things, and he did more than anyone expected him to."

"Yes, Mrs. Barrett and you taught him to be a kind, loving person, and a lot of us understood him and loved him."

"I know you did, and I love you for that. He thought he belonged to Mr. C. and Mrs. Leona, and later to you, as you belonged to C. H."

"You know, Mrs. B., Bubba may have saved my life. Do you really know he was the cause that Boyd Chalmers didn't catch me before I could get away from him?" Amanda asked.

"Yes, I think I knew, but I waited for him to tell me, and he never did," his mother said.

"I waited for him to mention it too, but I really believe he blocked it from his mind. He was so softhearted he couldn't stand to think of hurting anyone or anything—not even an animal—so I think he refused to remember he swung from a tree limb and caused that awful boy's death." And Amanda wept...again.

Then she said, "Don't you think the Lord had a hand in that and was gracious enough to see Bubba could forget it and not carry guilt around with him?"

And Mrs. Barrett said, "He is indeed gracious if He had that happen." And the two of them sat on with their thoughts and recollections.

Finally, the doctors came to tell them the surgery was over, the hot appendix was out, the cavity was irrigated, and they could do no more.

Dr. Story said, "There is a lot of infection left, and now it is in the hands of the Lord. Just remember, if he doesn't make it, it doesn't mean it is bad...a tragedy. Maybe Bubba's work may be over here. He touched a lot of our lives in a very positive way, and we must all be grateful for the years we have had with him."

Amanda and Mrs. Barrett sat by Bubba's bed in the waning hours of the day and left when John came at five to sit while they went to shower and have something to eat. Later, Mrs. Barrett went back to the hospital to sit and to relieve John. Then, at two, when Amanda could not sleep, she dressed and drove to the hospital to keep Mrs. B. company, as she remembered the wee hours were the most welcoming to the grim reaper—death. It was 2:25 a.m. when Bubba woke and asked, "Mama?"

And Mrs. Barrett said, "I'm here, Bubba."

And he said, "The flowers are bee-oot-i-ful, and there are so many. I wish you could see them. And Mr. C. is there; he is smiling and says everything is ready. And Mr. C. is well and happy." With those words he went up there, wherever it was that he was seeing, and he showed no fear whatsoever. And Mary Barrett and Amanda Halsey held each other and wept and smiled and told him goodbye.

The whole town paid tribute to that wonderful boy who had worked to make beautiful blooms brighten the Spartan existence of all the friends and neighbors, during the dark days of the 1930s economic depression. There were many flowers there at the service, and Amanda lovingly placed a perfect pink-and-coral bud he had grown in his pudgy fingers and told him goodbye again.

The minister from the Barretts' church made it very plain he believed Bubba had touched a lot of lives, in a very positive testimony to the ability of the Lord to help and bring solace to many. He said, "We should not grieve. We shall and should miss him, but you know he had an unworldly essence about him. I just believe it was time for him to take up again his unearthly work in a fairer and more perfect place. Too much grief is negative. The whining 'whys' and self-pity type, I believe, is never pleasing to our Heavenly Father, so suppose we all stand and lift our voices in joy and praise."

And so they did as they sang "To God Be the Glory." There were still some tears, but most of them were shining through the praise of the Lord.

Epilogue

John whistled, pounded on his desk, and looked at the clock just to see it was only three minutes since he had checked it last. Well, he hoped Amanda was all right. At noon she'd had twinges of a backache. This waiting and hoping she would have the baby soon and be back to being his well, the healthy, agile Amanda she had been a few months ago, was first and foremost on his mind. He hoped it would be soon, but the thought of her in labor scared him to death. They had been ecstatic when they had learned little Connor Halsey was on the way, but the closer the time came, the less enthusiastic he felt.

Finally, at fifteen minutes until five, he rose, put on his hat, and locked the office door. It seemed juvenile to be his age and unable to keep the office open regular hours. Just the same, he got into his car and drove home. After three and a half years, he could not be away from Amanda too long when she was *not* expecting a baby. Now it was next to impossible.

When he got home, she was sitting on the couch, painting her toenails.

"What are you doing with your knees under your chin, putting Connor in a close bind like that?"

She looked up, and he saw those marvelous, unique eyes were twinkling; her skin was beautiful beyond all reason, and he became dumfounded and wordless.

Then she said, "I'm trying to pass the time away until my pains get five minutes apart." And then she squinted up her eyes and pushed out big breaths.

He almost fainted. Then he said, "That's it, isn't it? Get yourself out there into the car. I just hope we have enough time to get to the hospital! Come on, Amanda, hurry! Why had you not called me?"

Amanda looked at him and giggled, when there was nothing funny to him going on here. She said, "John, settle down. Dr. Story has been here and says there is lots of time. First, let me explain that it would take a lot more than my knees to smash our little fellow. He is surrounded, insulated by pads of fat and fluids, something cushiony. Second, the doctor says for you to eat supper, as we could be in for a long night. First babies, he says, are usually not in a hurry to meet their parents." She put her feet down on the floor and said, "The little one says for you to fill up your tummy; you have time and his permission. Everything is all set to leave, and the hospital is ready for us when we get there. OK?" And of course, Amanda was right, so he forced himself to eat something; he never remembered what. He never remembered how he passed the time away until Amanda said the pains were right on time.

And she and the doctor were right. It was a long night, and John refused to leave her side. The nurse was horrified, but Dr. Story let him stay and coached him on how to help. There was no way the old doctor was going to tangle with a redheaded husband who was becoming a father for the first time.

The four of them—Doc, John, the nurse, and Amanda—spent a lot of time talking about different issues facing America with the war in the Far East and all of Europe. They wondered whether it would be better for John to enlist and take his commission or wait until the country asked for him to go.

Then, at 3:30 a.m., Amanda gathered her waning strength for one last heave, and John and Amanda became parents of a beautiful baby daughter. She was kind of wrinkled and splotched, but after John had seen and known what this little girl had gone through to land in his hands, he really did think she was beautiful.

Later, when the nurse got through changing the bed and giving Amanda a sponge bath, John, who had been helping the doctor clean, measure, and weigh the baby, brought the baby to Amanda, laid her beside her, and said, "What in the world are we going to name her?"

Then she looked at him and asked, "Wasn't your mother named Elizabeth?" He nodded, and she said, "Elizabeth, and maybe... maybe...Mary?"

"Not Evelyn? No? Mary Elizabeth? Sounds great to me. I know a lady named Mary who will be astonished but very pleased."

And both parents watched Mrs. Barrett closely when she was told the baby's name. She looked very puzzled and then looked at them with a question. They looked her in the face, nodded, and smiled.

Amanda thought, "If Bubba were here, he would be beside himself. He would ask when he saw her, 'Will she get bigger?' And her family would have said, 'Of course, she will!'"

She took time to remember Bubba. When he awakened sick that morning, he had been sick for days. He had denied being ill and had dragged about, declaring he was all right. When Dr. Story had seen him, he had been furious he had not been told. He had rushed him into surgery and seen the ruptured appendix and that the peritonitis was too far gone for the medicines of that day to have a chance to save him.

So he had been placed in the cemetery out close to Mr. C. and Mrs. Leona. Most of the town had been there to bid him farewell, and most of the floral offerings were made from the many flowers Bubba himself had grown, as the Connor flower garden had always welcomed folks who loved to harvest the many rosebushes. It had not been a very sad occasion, as most of what they all said was "Bubba has gone to heaven, and he is not by himself there, for Mr. C. and Mrs. Leona will show him around."

One of Mary Elizabeth's first visitors was her Granddad Hap, and he said, "This will be a whole new experience for me, as I've never raised a beautiful, bonny little girl. I am so happy; I had despaired of having *any* grandchild." And he seemed pleased with the little girl.

When John was sitting with the baby up against his neck and shoulder, barely moving a muscle, Amanda asked him if anyone had called Jessica. "Oh, yes," John said, "I think my dad called her, maybe the first of his many calls. I think he said she would be home next week, as she is doing finals right now."

Amanda said, "Well, her degree is only one full semester ahead of mine, because I will do my practice teaching next fall."

* * * * *

194

When everyone was gone for the night and Mary Elizabeth was fed and down for a while, John came to her bed and said, "Amanda, you have given me, finally, what I was put here on earth to do and have. I love you more every day. Everything you do is so wonderful. I may be a little jealous of little Livy with you, and I may be jealous of you with her. As you know, she will have complete and total use of the most ravishing parts of your body for a while. Do you think you can think of me part of the time when you let her use those gorgeous globes for what they were made for?"

She looked at him and said, "This little girl is going to be a big part of our lives from now on. I only love you more, because we have given each other something we hope will be a blessing, not to just us, but maybe to the world.

"She is, of course, just the beginning. In a year or two, we can begin to think about having Connor. Livy, as you call her, is going to have hair about the color of mine, I think, and for some reason, I keep seeing a skinny redheaded boy running around, aggravating his older sister."

"You will finish your degree and your teacher's certificate, but then these babies and I will need you home a lot until we start first grade. Will you be satisfied with the running of the store part-time, like you've done the last few years while you've been in school?"

"Yes, dear heart, I'll love every minute of it, and of course, Mrs. Barrett will be there to help with it all. I just wish Bubba could have stayed around a while longer to see the family grow. This baby would have amazed him. Wouldn't she?"

"Well, from what Doc said, his time was getting shorter because of the high blood pressure and weak heart, so we just have to place him up there with Mr. C. and Mrs. Leona. Do you think Livy would mind if I lifted her up, very gently, next to my heart?" And he looked guilty while he asked.

"No, I don't think she would mind, but why don't you just hold me there for right now? OK?" And it was OK. And Amanda's black-ringed eyes were telling him just how much he meant to her.

THE END

www.ingramcontent.com/pod-product-compliance
Ingram Content Group UK Ltd.
Pitfield, Milton Keynes, MK11 3LW, UK
UKHW040647260225
455582UK00015B/93/J